THE NEVER ENDERS

This book is a work of fiction. Names, characters, places, businesses, or incidents are products of the author's imagination or are used fictitiously. Any resemblance to actual events or persons living or dead is entirely coincidental.

An original publication of J. Boylston & Company, Publishers.

ibooks
1230 Park Avenue
New York, New York 10128
Tel: 212-427-7139 • Fax: 212-860-8852
bricktower@aol.com • www.BrickTowerPress.com

Library of Congress Cataloging-in-Publication Data

Sonbert, Michael.
THE NEVER ENDERS
ISBN: 1-59687-365-5
ISBN13: 978-1-59687-365-0
Library of Congress Control Number: 2008933424
Literary Fiction, Adult/General

Copyright © 2008 Michael Sonbert
First Edition
10 9 8 7 6 5 4 3 2 1

For my mom

This book exists, in part, because of the love, support and
encouragement of the following people. Thank you.

Peter Sonbert, Stacey Sonbert, Richard Kasher,
June Kasher, Marc Kasher, Jared Kasher,
Jackie Kasher, Olga Kasher, Esther Alix,
Dan Chayefsky, April Biggs, Deb Zaffron,
Lauren Maclise

All my friends at Landmark Education
All the coaches from the March 2002 S.E.L.P.
The Members of Voxvocis
The Members of The Biggs

John T. Colby Jr., for saving the day.

Randy J. Schaefer, the most patient woman I've never met.

Gina DeGregorio, PR Superstar

Bob Yehling, Editor Extraordinaire

I'd also like to thank
Roger Cooper, Maureen McTigue and Marianne Paul,
for hearing what I'd been screaming about for the
last three years.

Finally, I'd like to thank the real life Never Enders,
who've always welcomed me with open arms. You've
allowed me to stand beside you at the bottom of the world.
Here's to you finding your ladder.

I'm laying here drowning in my own blood, watching my best friend being pummeled by four guys with bleeding, burning, metal pipes, and the only thing I'm thinking is thank God they've stopped hitting me.

My mouth is blood and vomit and saliva. My left eye is nearly swollen shut but still I see Ginger, in all her hideousness, disappearing and reappearing inside of thick shadows and blood splatter.

Six days ago, death was all I wanted. It's why I came here. But lying here, crushed, jellylike, gushing on the floor of some roach-infested bar that doesn't matter to anyone, anywhere, I think about what it was like before all this happened. What it was like six days ago, before my experiments with self-destruction spiraled out of control.

Still, with everything that's happening, I'm smiling. I'm smiling about the thing that I know that none of them know.

THE NEVER ENDERS

by

Michael Sonbert

ibooks

NEW YORK

Perry

I sipped on a flask of whiskey I'd filled up from little tiny bottles I bought at the train station. Whiskey is funny. It tastes so sick and sour until you get used to it. But you have to admit that until you get used to it you're just drinking it to look cool. My flask is silver with two roses engraved on it. It was my dad's before he left. I named it Holly. I'd always heard about guys giving their guitars or sports cars old-time girly names, and since I didn't own either of those, I named my flask. I do cool shit like that all the time.

I liked being drunk. I'd been drunk off my ass for the last twenty-six days. That's twenty-six straight days of living inside a dream, only sobering up when I'd drink myself straight or when my whiskey would run out and I'd be too wrecked to make it to the liquor store. I was on a mission to destroy reality. My reality. The reality that it had taken me twenty-two years to come to terms with. The reality that I don't matter. That none of us matter. Most people realize on their deathbeds what I already knew. They're taking their last breath, wondering where it all went, realizing that their little speck of a life won't mean anything, ever.

Nobody matters. Nobody cares. Nobody is remembered. There is no future, no redemption, no hope. One day we will all be stuffed in caskets and thrown in the ground, covered with dirt and discarded, condemned to an existence as cold, flat photos in boring brown books on chipped, wooden coffee tables of people we've never met. Our friends and family will cry for a bit, if we're lucky, but soon life will go back to normal and we will be forgotten. One day we will all be dead, and we will be dead forever and nothing will be named after any of us.

The train burned through the countryside as the whiskey burned a whole in my chest. The biggest trees became memories outside my window. Gone. Left behind. Just like everyone I used to know. I reached into my pocket and held on tightly to the bottle of pink pills.

A girl with pale skin and glasses that covered light blue eyes smiled as she took off her backpack. She sat down across the aisle from me. She sat still, staring ahead. I watched her out of the corner of my eye. I made up stories about her. I always do that. I pretend that I can read someone. You know, what they're thinking or dealing with. It makes everything more interesting. I make up my own bullshit about someone because I always like my bullshit better than theirs. I even give them fake names.

I imagined that she was a bank robber named Charlotte who was on the run from the F.B.I. Charlotte used sex and manipulation to get what she wanted. But I thought she should really have turned herself in because there was no hope of ever truly being free on the run. Even if they didn't catch her, she'd never feel at home anywhere. She'd always be looking over her shoulder. It was sad, you know, everything about Charlotte. It was sad.

"What?" she asked turning towards me, causing some red-faced, white-haired man, who looked an awful lot like a giant pimple about to pop, to turn and look back at us.

"Nothing."

"Whad'ya mean nothing? You're staring at me." She looked me

up and down, checking me out. Pimple Head looked back again. I took a sip of Holly.

She pointed at my flask. "What is that?" She asked, whispering across the aisle.

"*What is that?*" I said laughing and imitating her. "It's whiskey. Do you want some?"

"It's four in the afternoon."

"So? Are you a Mormon or something?"

She shook her head at me like I was a bad child and then thought about it, super hard, for three seconds and said, "Give me some."

I handed it across the aisle to her. She smelled it, twice, and then sipped it. She nearly choked to death and her face turned so red I nearly died laughing.

"Oh my God…how…can you drink this?" she asked, in between coughs, as she struggled to catch her breath.

I shrugged my shoulders as she handed it back to me.

She tried to recover. She took off her glasses and rubbed her eyes. She inhaled, deep, then she yawned for a week and then I did also.

"What's with the notebook? Are you a writer?" she asked.

"No, it's a sketchpad."

That's another thing. I am always drawing. I'm kind of obsessed. My head is always buried in my sketchpad. I can draw my ass off —landscapes, the ocean (I've never seen the ocean except on T.V.), the sky. But mostly I draw people, the people that I meet.

"Looks like a notebook," she said. "But I'm blind without my glasses."

"Really?" I asked, and then did the international *jerking-off* motion to see if she saw it.

"Yeah, really. Look." She handed me her glasses and motioned for me to try them on.

People with glasses always make you try on their glasses, thinking somehow that the level of blurriness will totally blow your mind and you will realize how bad their eyesight is. Like anybody cares.

"Wow, pretty bad," I said, giving them back to her, blowing smoke up her ass.

I kept drinking. Ten minutes went by, at least. We didn't say a word but we kept looking at each other and then looking away real fast when we'd get caught, like we were ten years old or something. But one time, when I caught her staring, she didn't look away. She just smiled awkwardly, with her bottom lip shaking a bit. And then, her light blue eyes glazed over. The reflections of the trees screaming past, outside my window, skipped and popped off of her pupils as a few tears shimmered around the blue, pooling along the rim of her lower eyelids.

"Are you okay?"

"I am going to the city to see my boyfriend," she said out loud to herself. I just happened to be sitting there. "Do you have a girlfriend?" she asked.

"No."

"Are you a liar?"

"No. I don't have a girlfriend. I swear."

"Not about that, I mean in general. Are you a liar?"

"No, I don't think I am."

"My boyfriend is a liar. And right now I hate him more than I ever thought I could hate anybody."

We sat looking at each other for a moment.

"You shouldn't ever lie to someone you've said *I love you* to," she said and turned away.

I took a drink and leaned against the buzzing train wall with my head on the window. Charlotte changed shape slightly as her skin pulled tight and relaxed softly over her. She leaned back in her seat and closed her eyes. The sun shone in and caught her hair, face, and neck while she breathed deeply. Her breasts were small and pointy. I couldn't help thinking as I watched her inhale and exhale through her tiny nose and watched her eyes roll beneath painted lids that she was so little—about ninety pounds—and that if I punched her in the face as hard as I could, I'd probably kill her. I'd be doing her a favor. I lifted my fist and stared at it. I imagined smashing in Charlotte's face as she slumped deeper into her chair's belly. I'd stand over her and take a few practice strokes, lining up my shot perfectly. And then *boom!* Dead. Right there on the spot. What a powerful feeling. I'd be doing her a favor.

Charlotte slipped into her own thoughts as we sped away from a sun that was falling behind the trees. It was getting dark. The darkness always freaks me. It's like the universe is swallowing me in her black hands, pulling me into her black chest, smothering me, making me feel like I can't breathe. *I hate feeling like I can't breathe.*

A baby cried its little ass off. A kid with sticky fingers ran all over the place while his mother gave head to her lipstick. A guy with sick, oily skin and acne talked to the girl he was with much louder than he had to because he had headphones on and I held Holly upside down over my mouth as the last few drops of whiskey landed on my bottom lip and chin.

I was running out of oxygen. My shirt was tight around my throat and I couldn't swallow. I looked for something to throw through the windows in case I ran out of fake train air and needed the real kind. I saw a fire extinguisher, Charlotte's backpack, and that fucking kid who was still running up and down the aisle while his mother now applied her mascara. I stuck my foot out into the aisle; he tripped and stumbled over it. He shot me a wicked look and I stuck my tongue out at him. His clown-faced mother didn't see because she was too busy pretending to be somebody else. I didn't care anyway. I'd have spit on her.

I've always gotten a little freaked when I'm in tight, closed-off spaces, but lately, I'd been a fuckin' wreck. My doctor from back home, who is always clearing his throat, who always swallows his disgusting phlegm, who always makes me listen to him swallow his disgusting phlegm, who probably isn't fit to work on a cat's ass, gave me pink pills to take for when I get too freaked. I've never taken them. The whole bottle is in my pocket. I have them with me because when my money is gone and after I've drank myself nearly to death, I am going to rent a motel room, light up a cigarette, take a huge swig from Holly, and down the whole bottle of pills until my eyes close forever because fuck it, nobody cares.

I leaned my head against the window and stared out and up. The window was cold. It felt good on my face and head. I was exhausted. I imagined that I was an astronaut, hurtling through space, not afraid to be alone in the middle of nowhere. Not afraid of anything. I thought about my mom and how much I missed her already. I didn't even say goodbye. I yawned and closed my eyes. The world went dark. The darkness always freaks me. Still I fell asleep.

A young guy, probably about my age, with brown eyes and black teeth and clothes that didn't match was staring at me when I woke up.

"Hey, my name is Jason." He extended his right hand and waited for me to shake it. Jason, I thought, and laughed to myself. That wasn't his name. With those black teeth that looked like broken pieces of charcoal, I thought a better name for him would be Dirtmouth. Yes, that's what his parents should have named him, Dirtmouth. I shook Dirtmouth's hand. He had small, soft, girl hands that disappeared inside mine. I hated him for that.

"Heading to the city, huh?"

Dirtmouth was so smart.

"Yup." I gave him no room to say anything.

"Yeah, I got offered a job doing construction with my uncle so I figured I'd better jump on it seeing as how I need the money and all." He paused and pretended to scratch his nose but it looked to me like he was picking it. "I'm staying at a hostel over on Twenty-Second. Regent Palace, I think it's called. Where are you staying?"

I didn't answer.

"Plus I hear that there is a lot of sweet pussy in the city," he said.

Pimple Head turned and looked at me again. I shrugged my shoulders at him and laughed my ass off in my head because… c'mon… *sweet* pussy?

Dirtmouth started talking again. His mouth was a machine gun. He blew holes in my neck and head. I heard marijuana this and carpal tunnel syndrome that. Las Vegas this and Dave Mathews Band that. He was an escaped mental patient freaking out a few inches from my face. I looked around for another seat but the train was packed. I put my head down, ignoring him. I started to draw a picture of Pimple Head.

"Cool, you're an artist."

"Kind of…"

"…ever draw any naked chicks?"

"No...I've never drawn any..."

"Hey, you ever had sex with a midget?"

"No, have you?"

"Yeah man. It's cool as hell. You can throw her all over the place, like she's a doll or something."

I looked at him and smiled to see if he was joking but he kept a straight face, like he was serious as hell. "I've only had sex with one, but the one I did had the *sweetest* pussy ever. Like candy."

"Really?"

"Yup." He paused for a second and asked, "Have you ever had sex with an octogenarian?"

"No...I don't think so...what is that?"

"It's a chick that's over eighty years old. Like somebody's grandma."

"I don't think you can call a woman who's over eighty a 'chick.'"

"Either way, you gotta try it. You lube up that dry ass pussy and go."

"You got problems," I said.

"No way man. The old ladies, they know how to do it. They have the most experience." He burst into laughter that lasted a good two miles, but every five seconds he'd stop and stare at me. Then he'd laugh his ass off again.

"What's wrong with you?"

He was hysterical. "Yo man," he said. "I've never had sex with an old lady *or* a midget. I'm just messin' around."

He kept laughing like a black-toothed hyena.

"Nice," I said, shaking my head while he rubbed the tears from his eyes. What a bullshit liar.

He slowly stopped cracking up and breathed deeply, like he just got off. "Sorry," he said. "I have a habit of being a little over-anxious..."

"No shit."

"Yeah, especially when I'm talking to people I don't know. I kind of joke around because I don't really know what to say."

He looked at me forever, a little red-faced, like he was embarrassed, waiting for me to say something. He looked like a lost dog, all sad and lonely.

"The one about the eighty-year-old got me. I swear, you freaked me man."

He smiled big and checked his watch. "So what are you doing after we get in? You wanna get a beer or something?"

Dirtmouth seemed like an alright guy. He was an escaped mental patient and a bullshit liar but I didn't mind. I wasn't looking for any new friends but I figured I could invite him into my world. Whether or not he'd come would be up to him.

"After I get off this train, I'm gonna slide into the first bar I see, smoke a pack of cigarettes, and drink until I drop dead or pass out or whatever. You're welcome to come, if you're into that," I said.

The train dove and scared the moon off. My ears clogged as the tunnel swallowed us whole. A distorted voice gave directions from inside the ceiling.

I stood up, reached above my head, and freed my bag from the carry-on bag prison it had been in for hours. Others were swinging the doors open and freeing all the bags. It was a giant sock, toothbrush, porno-mag, and Q-tip jailbreak.

The train stopped. Frantic passengers bumped me as they ran to be first to get off and back to their exciting lives as census statistics. I threw an unlit cigarette into my mouth and attached to the fat crowd that pushed through the skinny train doors.

Dirtmouth was right behind me. "Hey man, you know you

never told me your name."

"I'm sorry…my name is Perry Patton. It's nice to meet you."

SMOKE

I stepped off the train onto cold cement being torn and mangled by 1,000 people wearing 2,000 shoes all going somewhere that, I guess, to them, right then, was the only place to be. A million sounds bashed my eardrums, disorienting and twisting me around… sounds of tired trains, gasping and sighing after long trips…sounds of eager trains, warming up, taking deep breaths in anticipation of the trips ahead. Hundreds of voices, saying very different things, combined to create a booming wall of sound that was much too high for me to climb.

A woman frantically looked for her idiot son. "John Paul!" she screamed in a high, shrill, burning voice. "John Paul! John Paul!" Her voice buried itself behind the backs of my eyes and tried to tunnel its way out. All these people, just like me, only different; not at all aware that there is no hope. Not at all aware that it will end the same for everyone—underground, trying to fight their way out from inside crowds that bottlenecked by staircases and escalators. People, just like me, only different, praying for the gravity of the crowd to lessen as we made our way towards the moon and the street and the living.

We walked together. We took the same steps. Everyone wanted to push ahead but feared the backlash. John Paul was still missing. I looked at all those people just like me, only different. They had faces with eyes that saw other faces with mouths, that spoke to other mouths on other faces, all with someplace to go or be, some with families, some without families, some with jobs, some looking for jobs, some with girlfriends or boyfriends or wives and husbands, or some looking for girlfriends or boyfriends to turn into wives and husbands. Some had dogs, cats, or kids, or none, or all…it didn't matter. It was fast, it was violent, and it wasn't going to have a happy ending for anyone.

I clutched my backpack to my chest and breathed. Each shallow breath made me more and more dizzy. *I hate crowds. They're the opiate of the co-dependent.* My stomach burned like hell from being empty. My mouth tasted like sandpaper and bleach.

The fat lady slob on my left that I'm sure doesn't stop eating, ever, and the skinny puke of a man to my right that looked an awful lot like a six-foot Pez dispenser, were holding me up. The escalators were close enough to touch. *I hope we all fall through and get caught up in the gears. That'll speed things up a bit.* Fifteen more feet. I couldn't breathe and I couldn't stand and people pushed the hell out of me. The unlit cigarette fell out of my mouth. John Paul was still lost. I couldn't turn back; if I fell down, I would have been crushed like the cigarette. I closed my eyes and got swept up in the flood.

Soon I was on my way to a new place. It was bigger and still underground, but somehow seemed safer. The escalator was bringing me there. Dirtmouth was behind me. He didn't seem to notice me freaking out. I started thinking about how he's actually not that bad looking until he opened his mouth and smiled. Man, his teeth were fucked. Some guy, about twenty-five, got off the escalator in front of us and started limping very slowly, causing everyone to bunch up at the top. They tried to get past him but made sure not to bump him and knock him down. I bet that guy wishes the whole world was escalators.

I was so thrilled to be away from the churning stomach of that building that I wanted to kiss the floor, just like an astronaut, not afraid of anything, who kisses the ground after he lands safely on earth because he is so happy to be home. Before he realizes that maybe he was better off staying in space because he hates his bullshit wife.

"Hey man, let's hit a bar and find some sweet pussy," he said.

I laughed a little. "Sure." I was trying very hard not to like him but it was tough.

With my bag on my back and Dirtmouth at my side, I stepped through the last doors and was born onto the screaming city street. The sky was cloudy. Even at night I could see it was cloudy. I felt the energy of the whole city inside me.

I twisted my neck up and around to see the tops of the buildings as we walked and he talked on the way to a bar we could get lost in. I made myself dizzy and nauseous so I would have to look away to center myself. When I felt better I would look up and do it again. Sometimes I think I like my life better when I'm sick and uncomfortable. That's when everything seems to make the most sense, when I'm sick and uncomfortable. I hoped that he wasn't offended that I wasn't talking. I *was* actually starting to like him but I'm not one of those people who has to constantly be talking to prove that he's still alive. I'm fine with silence.

We didn't walk into the first bar we found. We walked for a while. The one we stopped at seemed pretty crowded for a Wednesday night. Dirtmouth okayed it because it had a higher *sweet pussy* ratio. Everyone stared at us when we first walked in, but I didn't care. I killed them all in my head. I knew what their futures held. Dirt and headstones. The whole place was a cemetery.

No one at the bar moved out of our way at all, so we had to squeeze between a group of sorority-looking blonde girls to order our drinks. One girl spilled some of her drink on Dirtmouth while talking to her friends. They all laughed.

"Hey girls, it's alright. I didn't shower after my race today so it's okay," he said. "Yep, being a racecar driver sure makes you sweaty."

Oh man. This guy is a mental patient.

They laughed again, this time with him.

"Hey Perry, that's the sweet pussy I was talking about," he whispered.

"I see."

I ordered two beers and two shots of Jack. We slammed them. I ordered two more shots and we slammed them. I also ordered a double shot of Jack for myself as we grabbed our beers and made our way over to a small table in the corner of the room. Everything buzzed and my eyes watered as I scoped out the place.

Dirtmouth was antsy. "Hey man, let's go check out some chicks. All these girls man, they got sweet pussies."

"No thanks. But you can go."

I like girls as much as the next guy, but hitting on every girl in the place hoping that one will go home with me has never been my style. I just couldn't be bothered. Every once in a while though, I see a girl that I *have to* talk to and then I usually go for it.

She was on stage, about to speak. She didn't have a guitar. She was on her tiptoes to reach a microphone that was pretty low to begin with. She had a cigarette between the index and middle fingers on her left hand and a pad in her right. She looked up to the ceiling. I started sketching a picture of her. She made the pain in my stomach fade a bit. I stopped talking with Dirtmouth and began focusing completely on her. I'm not one of those people who has to constantly be talking to prove that he's still alive. Everything stopped buzzing. It just ended. All the noise, gone. She stood in the spotlight.

"This is called 'Cure Lonely,'" she said in an amazing, raspy-as-hell voice.

"*Cure lonely, when walls have faces/*
when dogs keep secrets/
and the stars in the night sky/
seem to throw the best parties."

Her voice was so deep and raspy like that actress whose name I can't remember.

"*Cure lonely, when disc jockeys tell me their life stories/*
When I'm sad in bed/
and he is everywhere but here."

She continued. She was alone. Just like me. We were the same. I watched the words dance off her tongue while she smoked and stared at the ceiling and smoked and smiled awkwardly and stared at the stage and laughed nervously and spoke under her breath. She stared over and around me and all of us into a place, I guess, where she would no longer be lonely.

The sound of a few people applauding brought me back into the room. She slunk off the stage and disappeared into the swarm next to the bar. I left Dirtmouth and tried to navigate my way through the crowd. I needed to meet this girl. She was lonely like me. She knew what it was like. She hurt. She hated. She was just like me. We were the same.

I arrived at the bar but didn't see her. I looked around at all the people who looked exactly the same. They were just like me only different. They still had hope. I sneaked in between a bunch of big shots and made my way towards the bathrooms. I called them big shots because they were wearing suits and talking very loudly, probably about stocks and takeovers and mergers. I hate guys like that. I am so glad that I am not one, although I do big-shot stuff sometimes.

I stood outside the woman's room for ten minutes hoping that she was inside. I was trying look casual but my suspicion is that I looked more like a pervert who enjoyed watching young ladies come and go from a dirty public toilet. She never came out.

I was crushed. I began to walk back to my seat with the feeling weighing on me that I just missed a chance to meet someone that I could destroy myself with.

Just then I heard soft, deep talking and whispering coming from an alcove near the cigarette machine. I peered inside. She talked into a payphone behind two poorly fitting glass doors. She smoked and cried softly. I watched her, hypnotized. I couldn't make out anything she said except for what she said as she hung up.

"Goodnight Jimmy. I love you."

Who the fuck is Jimmy?

She slid open the doors and I jumped back.

"Whoa, I'm sorry, I didn't see you there," I said, lying. She didn't say anything. "Hi," I choked out. "I just wanted to tell you that I thought your poem was pretty great." *Oh man, I am a dick.*

She just kind of stared at me.

"I don't know much about writing so my opinion doesn't mean anything but still I liked it." I didn't know what I was saying. I'm usually pretty cool around girls but not this time. I wanted to tell her that I understood her poem, that I felt like it was about me. I wanted to tell her that there is no *cure* for lonely. Lonely is forever. I calmed myself. "It was beautiful."

"What's your name?" she asked softly as she inhaled her

cigarette. Her voice was as deep as mine.

"I'm Perry. Perry Patton. What's yours?"

She started to come closer to me, into my space. She beckoned for me to lean down until my face was inches from hers. As she spoke, she exhaled two lungs full of smoke right into my eyes, making them water.

"Do you want to get out of here? You can come back to my place. It's just around the corner."

"Well, I'm here with my friend…kind of…so I'd just have to go tell him, you know, that I'm leaving."

She seemed uninterested as I spoke, not looking at me. "If you want to go, we've gotta go now. I want to leave. Call your friend in the morning."

She turned, walked toward the exit, and pushed open the front door. I followed.

Jimmy

I was lying naked in a strange place; a blanket covered my legs from my knees down. I was twisted on my side, facing the door, and as I looked down at my stomach as it heaved in and out, I thought to myself that I could probably stand to lose a few pounds. That's if I cared at all.

I was exhausted but clearly awake for the day. No new positions or sleeping techniques, even my latest that featured one pillow underneath my head and one pillow over, could get me to fall asleep again. At least I wasn't hung over. I never really get hung over anyway, and I drink like a maniac. I'm just lucky, I guess.

Buried beneath a mass of blankets, still sound asleep, was Smoke. That's what I named her after she blew a factory's worth of smoke into my face the night before. Her little olive-skined face was scrunched up. She didn't make a sound. And despite my wanting to run out of there because the idea of meeting her sober kind of freaked me, I stayed and stretched out long and thin and stared up at the ceiling.

Smoke was only the fourth girl that I'd ever had sex with. I had a girlfriend for three years back home. Her name, her *real* name, was Sarah. I liked her more than any girl I'd met up to that point, mainly because she was super nice and because she had long, blonde hair that always smelled like peaches. She's dead now because she had aneurysm on her brain. It was so sick. One moment she was cheerleading her little head off, and the next moment she was twitching and dying, laying facedown on the gym floor with her nose broken from the fall. I saw the whole thing, including the paramedics lifting her onto a stretcher with an oxygen mask slammed over her bloody face. She was dead already. I knew it. They had to do something though, because all the kids and players were freaking out. Anyway, that was four years ago, and forever minus four years leaves forever left to be dead. I'd doubt if anybody but me and her mom ever thought about her now. People forget. That's the way it is. Her mom always asked me to draw a picture of Sarah so she could have it framed but I never did because Sarah thought it was stupid. So what I did was I drew a picture of her when she was on the stretcher. I took out the stretcher and put grass beneath her to make it look like she was sleeping in a field. Even so it was still pretty hard to look at, at least for me, I guess, because I was trying to pretend. I brought it with me to the funeral. I thought I'd give it to her mom. But when I got there and saw Sarah in the casket and saw her mom standing over it, with black eyes, black from running mascara, black from misery, I decided I'd keep it. I walked out and never said goodbye to either of them.

After Sarah died, I screwed a couple of random girls while I was drunk off my ass but Smoke was the first girl in a while. She told me not to wear a condom because she said she wanted to *feel* me. She was pretty loud in bed, which I kind of hate because it's embarrassing and sounds kind of phony. Then there's the bullshit when the girl starts yelling that you are the best fuck she's ever had.

As she dreamt, I stood up, walked over to the window, and stole one of her cigarettes. The smoke flooded my lungs and calmed me. Normally I don't like people to see me naked because I have a big brown mole on my right ass-cheek, a mole that always kept me out of any high school mooning pranks; but she was out so... *Keys jingling outside the door...someone jiggles the lock...the knob turns...I inhale and hold it...I freeze...the door opens.*

In walked the most handsome and well put-together man that I'd ever seen, carrying a bag of what looked like groceries under one arm and a six-pack of beer under the other. Never in my life had I ever even acknowledged a man as being handsome. I guess I didn't even know what a handsome man was until I saw one. I couldn't believe my reaction; I thought I was turning gay. He had perfectly messed up jet black hair, and light, almost clear eyes. His skin was dark, smooth, and unblemished. His face looked like it was cut from stone or marble. Each and every line was perfect. Flawless. He noticed me as he put the bags on the counter.

I stood there naked, smoking. "What's up?"

I'm really not as cool as I pretended to be, but like I said, I do big shot stuff sometimes. My heart sank a bit as he looked me straight in the eyes. I was struck by the fact that he had the sickest yellow-green eyes I'd ever seen. The *only* yellow-green eyes I'd ever seen. Yellow-green like a poorly maintained front yard. That's ugly for a front yard, but looks beautiful on someone's face. I couldn't read him at all; I had no stories, no fantasies, no idea. We stood and stared at each other for a second. I heard a noise in the background; Smoke was waking up. I reached down and grabbed my pants.

"Good morning, Perry. Do you want some breakfast or maybe a beer?" He spoke softly.

Smoke walked in between us into the bathroom, completely nude. I felt myself turning red.

"Uh, yeah. I'll have a beer. No breakfast."

"Suit yourself, brother." He walked over and handed me a bottle. He twisted off the top while I held it. It tasted sick but I drank it anyway.

Who is this guy? Had I met him last night and forgotten? I wasn't that drunk. "Listen, I forgot your name. I mean, I was pretty drunk last night."

"I've never told you my name. In fact we've never even met before, brother," he replied, laughing a bit.

I liked the way he called me brother. "So how do you know me?"

He pointed to the bathroom and then to the telephone.

"What, she called you, last night, when I was here?"

"Yep. She called me two seconds after you passed out. Then she called me an hour after that. And an hour after that. Called me from the bar a few times as well."

I pointed my finger at him, taking a chance. "Jimmy?"

"You got it. James Dean Martin, in the flesh." He extended his hand for me to shake, his left hand. "Parents loved James Dean. Loved Dino Martino also. Named me after both of them. I prefer Jimmy though. Less pressure."

His voice was inside of me. It made me warm. It felt like, if the world was going to end and everybody only had fifteen minutes to live and they were freaking out and shitting in their pants and stuff like that, Jimmy's voice and Jimmy's presence could calm people down. I couldn't explain it, not yet, but I liked being around Jimmy.

Smoke came out of the bathroom in a robe. "Have you two met yet?" Her voice was so low it scraped the floor.

"Yeah, I was just offering Perry here some breakfast."

She walked by me like she didn't even know me.

"Last chance for eggs, brother. You sure you don't want any?"

"Um, okay, I'll have some." I reached for another beer. I was pretty hungry and my stomach burns if I don't eat.

"So what are you doing in town, Perry? You just come for the sex and the free breakfasts?" he asked, chuckling and looking at Smoke as she poured herself a glass of juice. She didn't look at either of us.

I smiled. "No." I didn't want to tell them why I was really there. Why depress everyone? "Just a vacation."

"Yeah? Who are you staying with, brother?"

"I'm staying over at a hostel on Twenty-Second. The Regent Palace." I lied. I didn't have a place to stay. That's where Dirtmouth said he was staying and it sounded alright. I figured I'd go check it out after I left there.

"So she got you into her clutches huh? You heard her read and you were hooked," he said with his back to me, cooking, while Smoke drank her juice in the other room, with the T.V. on.

"I really did love your poem," I hollered. "I mean that's just my *opinion* but you get enough people with the same opinion and…"

"…you get a holocaust," she yelled back.

I watched Jimmy make my eggs. I like to watch people when they cook for me. This way if they put poison in my food, I'll know to switch the plates after they've served them. Or maybe I'd just eat it anyway.

Jimmy put the eggs down in front of me along with a glass of juice that I didn't see him pour. I must've been daydreaming. "Enjoy, brother," he said as Smoke flipped channels.

"Thanks."

Smoke walked past me again into the bathroom. I didn't exactly expect her to be my girlfriend. Fuck, dead guys don't have girlfriends. But still she could've been a bit nicer. I was going to run out as soon as I woke up; instead, I stayed. She slammed the bathroom door. The sound of it shook me and the silence that followed made me sick to my stomach.

"Hey, man, do you think you could get me back to my hostel?"

"Oh that's easy. A few blocks away. I'll walk you right now if you'd like," Jimmy said.

I heard Smoke turn on the shower.

I couldn't believe she didn't even say goodbye to me. I yelled goodbye through the door but I don't know if she even heard me.

"She's messed up, Perry. Don't worry about it," Jimmy said as I kicked an empty soda can along the sidewalk. "She's the same with everybody. She was the same way with me when we first met. Now we're the best of friends. I've even got a key to her apartment."

Something about Jimmy made me feel better, more at ease. He knew things I didn't. Things I wanted to know.

He pointed at my pad. "So, what's with that?"

"It's not a notebook. It's a sketch—"

"Sketchpad, I know. Are you an artist?"

"Kind of. I draw. I can draw pretty much anything but I really love to draw the people I meet."

"Beautiful. So what do you have, like pages and pages full of pictures of everyone you've ever met?"

"Yeah, but I rarely look at the pictures after I've drawn them. I usually just want to see the person's face on the paper once. Then I'll remember it. Remember them. I don't think people should be forgotten."

He stopped and thought for a moment. "Okay, what about me? Draw me."

"Nah."

"Why not? You don't want to remember me?"

I was too embarrassed to draw him. He was so beautiful. What if I drew him and fell in love with him? Then I'd be gay forever. I'd have to start dressing differently and hanging out at different bars. It'd just be a big hassle.

"No, I'm too tired," I said smiling.

"Too tired, bullshit. C'mon, just do it."

I took my pencil out, flipped to a clean page, and began. He stood still for me. His eyes were yellow-green paint brushed in circles on vanilla ice cream. Delicious. It was so easy to draw him. All the lines were already made, perfect. I was just tracing over them. I felt the strangest sensations in my stomach and penis. He looked at me as I sweated out the alcohol. I finished up quickly and ripped it out.

"Here," I said, handing it to him.

"Wow. This is amazing."

He held it up next to his face so the whole world could compare the real and the less real. It did look an awful lot like him. "Can I keep it? It rocks."

"Sure. Really, you like it?"

He didn't answer. He just started walking again.

"This is your building, brother. Hey listen, tonight, why don't you meet us down at Cherry Bar? We'll all be there. And maybe you and she can talk about it, you know."

"Nah, I don't think so," I said. I wasn't trying to make friends. Friends might make me want to live and I didn't want to want to live. I liked having a cause; being a martyr.

"Jimmy, thanks for walking me back. It was real nice meeting you. Maybe I'll see you around."

"It was nice meeting you too Perry, and there's no maybe about it. Be at Cherry's at ten o'clock." He was smiling. His teeth were perfect.

"See ya," I said smiling back.

I got a room at The Regent Palace, which could have just as easily been called, *Shithole Arms*. The place was dilapidated; everything was brown and yellow and depressing as hell. There was no sign of Dirtmouth. I paid extra for a single room. It was up on the third floor and the place didn't have an elevator but it was the only single left so I took it. I wasn't about to share my room with any *Sick Fucks*. Sick Fucks is the name I made up for the people that'll smile to your face then stab you in your spine when you turn around. I've known a lot of them and they're everywhere.

I stepped in and closed my door. The room was small like an elevator. The bed was low and covered in dirty blankets and sheets. I walked to the bathroom. It was hot, like ninety degrees, and the water in the toilet was cloudy and up to the rim of the bowl. The shower was a box, hair clogged the drain, and a used razor sat on the ledge inside. I slammed the door shut.

I needed a place to hide my money: $4,600 that was left to me. I keep it in a shoebox. *After it's gone, so am I*. I opened the closet, pulled over a wobbly wooden chair, stood on it, and pushed slightly on one ceiling tile. It lifted. I put the shoebox inside and released the tile.

I opened my backpack and pulled out a sketchpad that I'd had since I was a kid. The cover was torn and wrinkled from years of being stuffed into this place or that. Most of the pages were no longer connected to the binding. Instead they rested, unattached, beneath the cover, ready and willing, and needing only a gust of wind to spill the story of my entire youth to any unfortunate passerby. I opened it and took out the two pictures I swore to myself I'd bring with me if I ever got to go anywhere. I pulled both out, unfolded them, and thumbtacked each one to the bloated wall next to the diseased bed.

I slept inside a thick soup, all day and hard as hell. Every time I tried to peel myself off the mattress to eat or drink a glass of water, which I desperately needed, or release the piss that I had been holding in for what seemed like my entire life and that by now, I was sure, had started leaking out of my bladder and into my body, starting to kill me, I couldn't. I was down for the day.

In and out of consciousness, I dreamt about a field with brown dirt and grass, with specks of green being torn and chewed by little children running. One of them looked just like me. The children ran and as they did some of them fell into holes in the ground and disappeared. Fire shot up from the holes like the kids got burned up. Soon it was just the little boy who looked like me, all alone, and the whole fuckin' field was on fire.

Ocean

The bar was so crowded I started to wonder how I would get out if a bomb went off, how any of us would. As flames engulfed most of us whole, people would get trampled and burned and melted, then cut open by the falling glass from the front windows that a fat, resourceful man chucked a barstool through to save us or himself or maybe just to get something to eat. We'd get poked in the eyes by a girl with long nails who was scratching and clawing at anything to keep from swallowing the devil. All to save lives that are not worth saving. Not at all. All these people, just like me, only different, changed from civilized martini-drinking swine to barbaric self-preservationists in a matter of seconds. I wonder if people *really know* just what they are capable of.

Dirtmouth was with me. I saw him in the lobby of the hostel. He grilled me about Smoke's sweet pussy and I gave him whatever details I could remember. I have to admit that I was starting to like him.

"Perry," I heard as I felt a strong hand drop onto my shoulder from behind.

It was Jimmy. He looked beautiful. "Glad you made it," he said softly. He said it softly despite the fact that everyone else was yelling to be heard over the music and the morons.

"Yeah, well, I didn't have any plans, you know, and I got kind of bored so I figured I'd stop by, or whatever," I said in a small, cracking, unsure voice pretending to be just the opposite. I introduced Jimmy and Dirtmouth although I did call Dirtmouth by his real name, Jason, because I'm really not an asshole.

"What'ya drinkin'?"

"Whiskey, rocks," I said.

"What about you?" Jimmy asked Dirtmouth.

"I drink vodka man, with some pineapple and cranberry juice."

"That's cute man. You should go put on a skirt," Jimmy said.

"Make fun if you want but that's how I get the sweet pussy to notice me. They come over and say (he imitated a girls voice), 'Excuse me, but can I have a sip of your deliciously fruity drink?' And I say, 'Sure baby. Do you mind if I stir it with my penis?' (back to the girls voice) 'Oh of course not. I insist on it.' And then I'm in. The sweet pussy can't refuse the penis parasol."

All three of us died laughing.

My drink tasted like fire in my throat as Jimmy grabbed my shirt sleeve and began to navigate his way through the cattle; Effortless. Dirtmouth followed. I don't think Jimmy touched a single person on his way to a cramped table in a lightless corner of the room. The darkness always freaks me. He pulled out chairs for both of us and as we sat he did as well. Smoke was there. She glanced at me. Also there was another guy that looked older than me, although it was hard to tell through the thick bar haze.

He had a tattoo on his neck of the words "love life" written in a clean, skinny, black writing. I thought it was bullshit. *Love life.* *Fuck life.* At least it must've hurt like hell. I could relate to that. I could relate to someone hurting and scarring himself even if I thought the message was crap.

The thing about this guy, other than the tattoo, was that he was huge. Even sitting down I could see it. His shoulders were so wide I doubted he could walk through the doorway without turning sideways. Even sitting down, he looked as if he was standing. Jimmy introduced us and we shook hands. His hands were rough as hell.

Drinking my whiskey, getting drunk off my ass, I so loved watching and listening to them. Especially Jimmy. Man, he had the whole place wired. He was like the mayor. Girls, guys, the bar staff, everyone knew him; they treated him like a king. We were his court. Just sitting with him gave me a respect that I'd never felt before.

He smiled at me and asked, "You enjoying yourself, Perry?"

"Fuck yeah."

He *was* King. That would be a good name for him if I didn't like calling him Jimmy so damn much. *King.*

"Hey man, there are some girls for you," Jimmy said to Dirtmouth, talking about three girls who had sat down at the next table. Dirtmouth had been running all over the place since we'd arrived, talking to all the girls in the place and getting rejected by all of them. Seriously rejected. Laughed at. He didn't care. That's something I really liked about him. He didn't care.

"Oh shit. Some sweet pussy sitting down right next to me. Don't they know that once I get them in my sight they have no chance?"

He was holding his hands up like he was looking through the scope of a gun. He was so fuckin' funny.

I started to get my nerve up. I wanted to talk to Smoke all night but I wanted to get drunk off my ass first, so I wasn't as tense. Like I said, I'm not really shy when it comes to girls, but this one really freaked me. My stomach felt so fuckin' sick when she looked at me.

I slid my chair over next to hers and caught a glance from Jimmy. He smiled. She turned away from the big guy to look at me. I'd interrupted their conversation but I didn't care.

"Listen," I said. "I was wondering if we could talk about last night. You know and about this morning and how you acted... towards me and everything."

She just stared at me, smoking as always. Jesus, she freaked me.

I went on. "I kind of thought that maybe we could hang out again or something. You know if you wanted."

My hands were sweating and I felt my face turning from the pinkish red that I was sure it had been from the start of the conversation to more of a purplish color as she said a roomful of nothing and left me dangling out on the ledge of awkward silence.

Jimmy and the big guy were talking but also, I suspect, eavesdropping. Dirtmouth was talking to the "sweet pussy" at the adjoining table.

Then Smoke did something that I hadn't seen her do since we'd met. It had only been one day, I know, since we'd met, but most people do this *at least* once a day and in most cases much more. She smiled. She smiled right at me and I smiled back.

"Perry, I'm sorry if I gave you the wrong impression," she said, hoarse as hell. "I was very depressed last night and you came along and you were nice to me. I mean, you were genuinely nice to me. I needed the company and it just happened to be you. But it could have been anyone. I want you to understand that."

Boom.

"Now, if you want to be friends that's fine. But I can't have some little puppy dog following me around all the time. We're never going to be intimate again. It was a one-night deal."

I broke. My insides, I heard them. They broke. I didn't know why the fuck I even cared. I didn't even want a girlfriend. Shit, I'd be dead soon. Still, I always felt like garbage when people didn't like me as much as I liked them.

She smiled again and I focused my eyes inside my glass and watched the last bit of ice melt away. It tried to hang on but it just couldn't.

Jimmy jumped up and the commotion brought me back into the room. "Let's go, Perry. You're coming with me."

I was too drunk to go anywhere, but still I stood and followed. Smoke, the big guy, and Dirtmouth followed as well. We walked through an invisible door in the back of the bar you would have to know was there or you'd never see it. We plodded, with the walls holding at least me up, through a maze of hallways that all looked exactly the same. I was still reeling from the blow Smoke had dealt me and was having trouble looking at her.

We arrived at a beige door that must've just recently been red because in some areas where the paint was thin, the red was seeping through, like blood beneath skin, trying to get out. Jimmy pushed open the door and Smoke and the big guy walked into the room. Jimmy nodded at me and Dirtmouth and we walked in as well. He came in last and closed the door behind him.

There was a boring wooden table in the middle of the room with five equally boring chairs. Smoke sat in one, the big guy another, and Jimmy the third. They watched us, waiting to see if we'd sit or just remain stuck to the wall. Again Jimmy nodded to us and then to the empty chairs. I walked over to mine and pulled it out. Dirtmouth did the same. Smoke smiled again and the big guy clapped his hands softly and slowly. I sat down, pulled my chair in and turned to Jimmy. I lit a cigarette.

I watched the big guy, his face revealed in this room now that the light shone on him. He stared with steady brown eyes and a coarse, jagged, unshaven face that seemed to have more experience than the four of ours together. He wasn't necessarily ugly, but he wasn't all that good looking, either. He was kind of like me except he had that *I may be a mass murderer* look going for him. I think girls like that. They all say they want a nice guy, but that's bullshit. They all want someone who will treat them exactly how they feel—like shit. The guy was so damn big. He was massive, I'd say six-foot-six, maybe two hundred thirty pounds. He looked dangerous and he was rough as hell. He was Ocean. That's what I named him. I wished I'd brought my pad.

Jimmy reached into his pocket and pulled out a cellophane bag with white powder in it. My heart jumped because although it looked like beautifully packaged snow, I knew exactly what it was. I'd never tried coke before. This would be my first time.

"Oh shit," Dirtmouth said. "A little sugar, what did I do to deserve this?"

"You're a friend of Perry's. It's that simple," Jimmy replied.

I guess I must've had a fucked-up face on because Jimmy asked if I was alright.

"Yeah, yeah. I've just never done blow before."

"Blow," Smoke said and laughed. "Are you from the seventies Perry?"

"Perry, it's not a big deal," Jimmy said as he poured some coke out and began crushing it with a credit card. He laid the card on top of the coke, then pushed it down and back and forth until the rocky chunks became smooth and clean. He separated it into five lines, each about two inches long. "But you don't have to if you don't want."

I was pulling hard on my cigarette, smoking my ass off.

"Can I lick the card?" Dirtmouth asked reaching for it.

"That's why your teeth are so fucked up," Ocean said as Jimmy handed Dirtmouth the card.

"No, my teeth are fucked from eating too much nasty pussy. That's why I only go for sweet pussy now," he said. He licked the filthy card from one side to the other.

Jimmy took out a hundred-dollar bill and rolled it up into a tight little cylinder. He handed it to Smoke while watching me. She leaned over the table, put the bill in her nose, and inhaled an entire line. She leaned back and pulled hard on her cigarette. Ocean inhaled his line and Dirtmouth did the same. Jimmy handed me the bill.

"It's okay," he said.

Suddenly, I started thinking about my mom, like I'd be letting her down if I did it. I didn't know what I was afraid of. Dying? Like my life was so great. It was just a pointless, bleak march towards a freezing, pitch-black forever. So what if I let mom down? Fuck it. Fuck everything.

I leaned down and put the rolled bill in my right nostril. It rested snugly inside. I felt them watching as I positioned myself above my line. I began to inhale but must've blown out a little because the coke spread out and covered the table like winter snow on a frozen road. They all laughed. Jimmy fixed the line with his card and Dirtmouth licked it again. As I leaned down Jimmy said, "Don't breathe out Perry."

People that don't *breathe out* are dead, I thought as I inhaled the entire thing.

There was no sound. No movement. No life. I sat frozen, like a mannequin, with fake plastic eyes in a room where forever and never kiss and are one in the same. At that moment, I truly did not exist.

And then with a crack as loud as an A-bomb blast, I was back inside real life and that room and my skin. I felt my throat close, my stomach clench like a fist, my ears fill with screaming blood, and my nose burning fire. I'd just inhaled every chemical under the sink in my mother's house and I could taste them in my mouth and my throat.

Jimmy snorted his line. I was dizzy. Dirtmouth was talking. Smoke, smoking. Ocean, laughing. I jumped up and started dry heaving violently. I felt my insides wrenching.

"In the garbage, in the garbage," Smoke yelled.

I ran to the garbage and slipped, slamming my throat on the rim of the pail. I vomited from my knees with my mouth at pail level. The puke splattered off the inside of the can and back into my face. It spit back into my eyes and hung from my lashes while some got caught up behind the back of my nose. I coughed and drooled as the smell of the puke trapped inside my nasal cavity made me sicker. I blinked and matted my lashes with puke. I heaved again and more vomit shot from my mouth and nose. Jimmy bent down and started rubbing my back.

"Hey brother, it's totally normal. Don't worry about it," he said.

The fresh air running through the streets felt alive in my lungs and on my eyes. Everything was buzzing. I was grinding my teeth.

It was just Jimmy and me stumbling away from the bar. Ocean had evaporated and Smoke burned away. Dirtmouth actually found some girl that seemed interested in him, so he stayed. He put his thumbs up and said "Hey" like he was *The Fonz*, as we walked out. I really liked him a lot.

The voices in the dark on the sick street attached to each

other and funneled down my throat, killing me before I could remember that I was dead already. We were silent for most of the walk back to the hostel. My mind was racing a million miles an hour. I had humiliated myself. We stood outside.

"Jimmy..." I was interrupted before I could finish.

"Perry, why are you staying in this shithole? Don't you know someone here in town that can put you up?"

"Well my…my brother Alex but…"

"You have a brother? Does he know you're here? Do you have his number?"

"Yeah, I do. I thought about calling him but I don't want to be a bother."

Alex is eight years older than me and we *do not* get along. He left home about seven years ago and I swear we've only spoken ten times since and only seen each other once and that was twenty-eight days ago. He left because he said he hated living in a small town, but I just think he couldn't deal with things after dad left. We never got along, mostly because he was much older and really didn't want his little brother tagging along with him and his big shot friends.

Also, he was crazy into all that self-help shit, and was loaded down with audio and videotapes of people telling him that he *is an unstoppable force of nature.* They ran, twenty-four seven. It's called a mantra. And when you repeat it enough, you either believe it or you make it true. Every time I walked past his room I'd hear, "I am an unstoppable force of nature. I am an unstoppable force of nature."

After he left, mom cried for weeks. First dad took off and then Alex, six months later. She was as sad as anyone could be and I hated both of them for that.

He did make something out of himself. He is a super bright

super lawyer and he is only thirty years old. He is a total big shot. I guess those mantras worked. He's had a girlfriend forever. She's a writer. She works for a pretty big magazine. She's always been super nice to me. In fact she's offered to get me an interview at her magazine a couple of times for some kind of bullshit go-fer work, but still working just the same. She offered after I quit my job at the pet store back home and refused to work an uninspiring job ever again. I do big shot stuff like that sometimes. Like being a go-fer is so damn inspiring. I think she just wanted to bridge the gap between me and Alex. She's really nice like that. I thought about calling them when I came here but didn't really want to be a bother. I felt like Alex made a choice to be rid of me a while ago. The last thing he needed was his younger brother hanging around with him and his new life.

Jimmy put his hand on my shoulder. "Go in and get some sleep."

"Well when will I see you again? I mean all of you."

"I'll come calling. Go in. It's gonna be light out soon."

He hugged me and walked away.

I nearly collapsed by the time I reached the top of the third-floor steps. I dragged my feet down the hall to my room and the door was open. I knew I didn't leave it open. I never leave doors open. I check them thirty fuckin' times so I'm sure I'm not leaving them open. I heard some noise coming from inside. I peeked in and the door slammed into my head, knocking me down. It blew open and a guy in all black with a black ski mask ran out of my room and right at me. I put my hands up but he kicked me in my stomach. I doubled over and he kicked me in my head three times. I curled up in a ball and lay there. I couldn't catch my breath.

I looked up and he was gone. All I kept thinking was that he stole my money. I crawled through the door and hobbled over to the closet. I pulled a chair over and climbed on top of it, holding my stomach. I found the shoebox inside the ceiling tile. It was fine. Untouched. My bag, that I'd left on my bed, was wide open and everything was thrown out of it. What a sick fuck.

My head was ringing.

I locked the door and sat on the bed. Outside the window, the day began. It was still dark but dark from clouds not nighttime dark. My heart beat fast and my stomach hurt from being kicked and from being empty. I put my clothes back into my bag unfolded. Everything seemed to be there except for my flask, Holly. I guess that was kind of stupid to name that thing anyway. I looked at the two pictures I'd hung on the wall, the two pictures I swore I take with me if I ever went anywhere. One was the first picture I'd ever drawn. It wasn't very good but that wasn't what was special about it. It was a picture of me, my mom, my dad, and Alex. I copied it from a picture that our neighbor took of the four of us after Alex's high school football team won the State Championship. He was eighteen and I was ten and we were all happy. I knew Mom and Dad had problems before, but after that it seemed like everything started falling apart. I took the thumbtacks out of both pictures, folded them, and put them inside the old sketchpad. I took the shoebox and the pad and stuffed them in my bag and threw it over my shoulder.

I could've easily left without making a scene or being a prick but I didn't. I usually never do. I walked down the steps and into the kitchen.

A young woman worked behind the counter.

"Can I have two dozen eggs please?"

"In an omelet?"

"No, just two dozen eggs, not cooked. I'll pay the cooked eggs price," I told her.

I walked back up to my room. I cracked eggs under the mattress. I cracked eggs under the sink. I lifted the ceiling tile in the closet and threw eggs in every direction. Some only went a few feet but some rolled at least down the hall and above the other rooms on the floor. Most cracked, which is what I wanted. In a few days, it would start to smell like the end of the world up there and no one would know why. When they did find out, all I could say was, *Good luck cleaning rotten egg off the inside of the ceiling, assholes.*

ANDREA

I pulled hard on my last cigarette as I sunk deep inside my jacket. It was raining softly and quietly, and I was freezing. People pushed past me on their way to work. I bounced from Big Shot to Big Shot, stealing their energy and leaving them desperate and still dying without them even knowing it. I stopped in front of a deli. I hadn't eaten since my two-egg breakfast with Jimmy the day before. I didn't care. The searing pain in my belly had become my friend, accompanying me wherever I went. I felt like I didn't need to eat or drink anything. Food became dirt and horseshit, laced with evil; drink turned to kerosene and battery acid, flooded with poison. I only needed alcohol and cigarettes.

I sat down and put my bag between my legs. I pulled Alex's number from my pocket and began flipping it from finger to finger.

"Hi, this is Alex. I can't get to the phone right now but if you leave me a message I will call you back."

"Hi Alex…it's Perry. I'm in the city and I wanted to…uh…say hi, so uh I'll call you back…"

"Perry? How are you, it's Andrea!"

Andrea is Alex's girlfriend. I already mentioned about her writing and about how super nice she is about everything but I never said that she has huge tits; she's hot as hell.

"I'm good. I'm in the city for a few days or a week, whatever, and wanted to say hi."

I really needed a place to stay and I didn't feel comfortable staying at another hostel, seeing as how there are Sick Fucks everywhere when it comes to those places. And Alex told me twenty-eight days ago to call him if I ever needed anything. I think he felt bad for me seeing as how I was so depressed, but fuck it—he said it, so I called.

"Okay, I'm on my way out the door. I'm late for work. Alex is on his way home from a business trip. Why don't you meet me over at my office? I'd love to introduce you to everyone."

I washed my face and hands in the bathroom sink in the corner diner by her office. I sprayed on some cologne to cover up the fact that I hadn't showered in a few days. I didn't really care for myself but figured she'd be embarrassed if all the Big Shots at her office thought I smelled like vinegar and ass-crack.

My stomach growled so loudly I threw down a blueberry muffin to avoid grossing the shit out of some Big Shot she worked with. Some Big Shots get grossed out easily.

We met on the corner. It was 8:15.

"Perry, how are you?!" She asked, happy as hell to see me.

I'm dead and so are you. "I'm fine...I'm great."

I can pretend that I'm great even when I'm not. It's a talent. If you don't have it, you really can't learn it.

"Are you sure?"

I cleaned up pretty nicely and I think I smelled fine, but no matter how good you are at pretending you are fine, your eyes will always give you away. It's the one thing in this whole world that I know. Your eyes will always give you away. I think mine gave me away.

"I didn't know you smoked," she said.

"I just started about a month ago."

I didn't care if I got cancer. It would give me a reason to care about life the way it does with most people who get it.

GRAVITY ROOM

There were people crowded in the doorway smoking and talking, I think about me, as Andrea slid and I contorted past the bodies on the way into her building. I'd have spit on all of them, if the mood had struck me.

The chatting mob at the mouth of the elevator lost its voice as we stepped on and it made me realize something: People don't talk in elevators. Or if they do, it's so quietly and so briefly as not to be noticed at all. Little mice squeaking and twittering, rubbing shoulders with the rest of the vermin. In an elevator the self-conscious rule.

I think they should make the inside of movie theaters look like the inside of elevators. Maybe then people will shut the fuck up while you're trying to watch a movie. A movie that sucks but one you're watching anyway because you spent the money on the ticket and because you're hoping it gets better. I mean, it *has to*.

The tension rose with each floor we passed. The air became more solid than gas, a wall of thick, transparent stillness surrounding each of us. I felt the gravity room was near. I felt like I was going to faint.

The neon colors over the doorway smacked my eyes like the flash from a bomb as we stepped off the death lift at her floor. I saw the sign: G3. *Girl Got Gravity*. That's what the sign read. That's her magazine.

There were so many people talking at once it was confusing,

until my ears readjusted themselves and made sense of it all. Like when you're at a football game and a thousand people talking sounds like a thousand people talking until the big screen says something like *CHARGE!!* Or *DE-FENSE!!* and slowly but surely, as everyone catches on and starts to repeat the phrase, the words make sense and everything is okay. Well, until some fat Big Shot spills a soda on you and his friends laugh and you don't say anything.

Andrea was a pretty big deal down there. It's the only reason why she was allowed to bring me up. She could do pretty much whatever she wanted. She's the one who landed the Roger Thompson interview, the one when he admitted to experimenting with homosexuality in college. That all but killed him in the election. Anyone who was on the fence went with the other guy and Thompson, well, he went home. Maybe with a man.

As I followed Andrea through the room and watched the way she spoke to and listened, really listened, to everyone, and as she introduced me to a bunch of Big Shots whose names I had already forgotten, I wanted, just for a second, to kiss her on her mouth.

We walked into her office. She turned to me. "Do you want some coffee?"

"No thanks."

We stared at each other for a minute until she asked, "Hey do you want me to see if my boss can meet with you?"

"Uh…" I didn't. I didn't want some bullshit job. I didn't come here to be put on the spot.

"C'mon Perry, it would be so great if you worked here. You could totally move to the city. You should meet with him."

"Sure," I said, not wanting to disappoint her. I just hoped he was too busy to see me.

She disappeared for about five minutes. I thought about spitting in her coffee. Not for any reason other than I just felt like it.

"Perry, he said he'll see you."

I didn't want to meet that guy or even be there at all. I should have stayed at the hostel with the Sick Fucks. Either way, I wouldn't go back there now. The whole place was gonna reek because some psycho put broken eggs everywhere.

Andrea led me into his office. She sipped on her coffee and I felt happy that I didn't spit in it. I'm really not an asshole.

"Perry, pleasure to finally meet you. Andrea speaks very highly of you," said a man with a tie and a suit and a long, slim face and curly, brownish hair who looked like he was in his early forties.

"Hi Sir, thanks for meeting with me."

I love calling Big Shots "Sir." It really gets them off.

I looked on his desk at a picture of what looked like a very happy family. I wondered, however, what secrets they had.

He spoke and smiled in front of an enormous bay window that overlooked the entire city. And although I had just met him, part of me wanted to push him through the glass, just to see what would happen.

"Okay, Andrea, you can leave us," he said, motioning to the door and sitting down at the same time.

"Sit, please!"

He was still smiling wide and it kind of threw me. I was always suspicious of the smiling. I mean, what are they up to?

"Perry, Perry, Perry," he said, like we were best friends or old army buddies. "So good to finally meet you. I have heard so many good things, I knew I had to get together with you in person."

"Really?"

Who said good things about me? Andrea? Why?

"Yes really! You're a pretty great guy from what I hear. We might have something over here for a guy like you."

A guy like me. What did that mean? There are other guys like me. An army of suicidal, self-destructs who've given up hope? Like we're a club or something? Like The Boy Scouts only instead of helping old ladies across the street, we push them into traffic.

"Well, why don't you tell me a little bit about yourself. You know, we'll get acquainted and then maybe we can talk about setting something up for you."

Well I fuckin' hate you and I'd love to bash your brains in with this chair. That's about it. Oh, also I'm going to kill myself this week. Am I hired?

He spoke very calmly. But also very sneakily, saying things like, "*a guy like you*" and "*we can talk about setting something up.*" He was the ultimate Big Shot. He droned on for about ten minutes about his hometown, his ex-wife, Doris, his magazine, and French bulldogs. He loved them and I didn't feel strongly one way or the other.

All I knew is that I hated *hot* dogs. Once, when I was a kid, I ate one at a fair they had a few towns away from mine, back home. As all the inbreds limped from booth to booth wasting money on impossible games in an attempt to win stuffed monkeys and bears, I laid on the grass with the diseased hot dog I had just eaten attacking every organ in my body. The infection spreading, the paramecium bathing in my blood, killing me as I writhed in pain in front of a toothless gaggle of demented onlookers. Sweating and hallucinating, I reached out at all the faces, fake and real, trying to peel the skin back to reveal the metal and the wires. Until finally the demon freed itself in an orgy of vomit and diarrhea right there on the grass in front of everyone. I've never eaten a hot dog since and probably never will. Anyway, it was probably the most exciting thing that happened to anyone that day, until they all went home and shoved beer bottles up each other's asses or whatever they did for fun.

"So," he said.

"So?"

"Perry, um, what is it you want to do?"

"What do you mean? Here? For you?"

He paused. "No, I mean overall, in your life. What really lights you up?"

He smiled like a retard.

"I don't know. I never thought about it." I knew it didn't matter what I did or what anyone did. It was all just passing time before *time* was all there was.

"Well. What if I gave you a job?"

"Okay," I said suspiciously.

"What about it? A job, at a major magazine. That's pretty cool. Right?"

"Yeah, I guess. But doing what?"

This guy was the *epitome* of the term *Big Shot*. What a bullshit liar. You don't offer someone a mystery job—especially someone who isn't qualified to do that mystery job. Whatever it is.

"We'll figure it out. Come in on Monday."

He said it while looking towards the glass window that connected his office to the hall. I turned and saw Andrea standing there talking to someone else. He was staring at her.

"Yeah, but why?"

"As a favor to Andy."

Andy. That's what he calls her?

I coughed and he said, "*God bless you,*" like I sneezed. I didn't correct him. I can be a pussy sometimes. Especially around someone older than me

"So, I just come in and that's it. *We'll figure it out*," I said, getting uptight. My stomach was starting to hurt. I felt like I was going to have diarrhea.

"Yeah. That's it. We can have you down in the copy room or in the mail room. Something to get you in action. Something to get you started in the real world. So what do ya think?"

My silence forced him to repeat himself.

"What do you think, about the offer? You know, like I said, to start in the copy room and see what happens. I mean you never know, maybe even one day you could be sitting in my chair."

I felt sick. The muffin or all the booze caught up to me right then. I clenched my butt cheeks to avoid having to shit my pants. I wanted to tell this guy to fuck off. I was freaked by him, though. Some Big Shots really intimidate me. They speak in a very confident way and it freaks me. It'd be better if I just accepted and never showed up. That's what I'd do. I needed to find a bathroom. I could feel a little bit of diarrhea run out of my ass and down the back of my balls.

I accepted the job offer. I didn't have the energy to fight that fuck anymore. We shook hands and I walked out of his office, slightly hunched holding my stomach and clenching my ass. I knew I'd never see him again. I couldn't help thinking, though, as I said goodbye with a fake smile painted on my beaten face, that I should have gone with my first instinct and pushed him out the window.

Andrea congratulated me with a huge tit-squishing hug and kiss that nearly caused me to crap my pants in front of everyone.

"Perry, do you need a place to stay?"

"No…no…I'm cool. I'm staying with some friends from back home. They have a place downtown."

I knew she didn't believe me because after I said it she looked immediately at my bag. Why would I have all my stuff with me if I had a place to stay?

"Okaaaay… But you have our number in case you change your mind."

"Yes."

"Perry, please don't hesitate to use it."

"Okay."

"See ya Monday."

She really is very sweet.

Ginger

I needed air. Lots of it. Like an overdose. It was windy on the street as I walked, letting the wind push me around, feeling sorry for myself. I pulled so hard on my cigarette my lungs felt like they were going to blow up inside me. I drank whiskey straight from a liter I'd bought at a store on the corner. Each swig sent chills through my entire being and after each one I vomited a little bit, caught it in my mouth, and swallowed it. It was sour and evil. As I danced with the people walking towards me, I hoped that it didn't upset Andrea to see me. I tried to look happy, for her.

Here are my mantras: *I am hopeless. I am chipped paint peeled away. I am the walking dead. I cannot be saved.*

I dragged my feet for blocks, in everybody's way as always, with thoughts and ideas racing through me. Stopping just long enough to get me interested and leaving the same way everything leaves, with me sad and wanting more but knowing that there is nothing more.

I sat down on a bench and watched all the people I didn't know and never would. People that didn't matter to me because I didn't know them. It got me thinking about everybody I'd ever loved. They all could have been anybody. *Everybody everywhere is exactly the same. Nothing is different.* The only reason why I'd felt any affinity for the people in my life is because they're the ones I'd met first.

No matter. I cannot love any more.

Time fell away as I sat on the bench that had frozen and

numbed my ass. I swear I couldn't feel a thing down there. I thought that now more than ever, more than any time in my whole life up to that point, now would be the best time for me to get shot in the ass by an assassin who was trying to kill someone important but hit me instead. I would be declared a hero. And only I would know if I really meant to block the bullet or if it was just dumb luck as I bent over to tie my shoe.

My mind was away as usual when she walked out of the dust. She glowed and shimmered as the sun flickered through the trees and buildings down on her. She turned from light to black, angel to demon, in the same step. She came closer to me, bringing the sun and the moon and placing them all in my lap for me to hold. As she walked past me, her blood asked me to fall in love with her a thousand times over. I was just born to her and I would die for her. And as she walked into the coffee shop I imagined that she turned and looked right at me and blew me a kiss. I imagined that she blew me a kiss that I think I caught but can't be sure because blown kisses are always invisible.

I was interrupted by a tennis ball and a slobbering dog, I think a yellow lab, landing on my lap. He was clearly taking his master for a walk, not the other way.

"I'm sorry about that. C'mon Steve, lets go, c'mon," said a man, out for his afternoon walk.

His dog was still up on my lap. I didn't really mind. He seemed like a nice dog.

"No problem," I said.

"C'mon Steve. C'mon, let's go."

The dog lost interest in me when he remembered his master's voice. He jumped down. He left me. I felt sad.

The dog was slathering his master's face and at some points, his mouth. His tongue darted in and out. The whole scene struck me as being oddly homosexual. The dog's name was Steve, which is first of all retarded. Why name a dog after a person when there are millions of really cool dog names out there?

"Oh yes Steve. You're a good boy. Yes."

Oh man, what the fuck was I watching? Steve and his master were really getting into it. The two of them, expressing their homosexual, man-dog love in public, for the world to see. It turned my stomach. Just like pornography. I couldn't stop watching, though. Just like pornography.

"Oh, you're a good boy, aren't you?"

Steve was a good boy. Well at least he thought so. But I mean, a man, having a man pet, and then naming him after a human man? Weird, seeing as how there are a ton of really cool dog names out there. None of which I can think of right now.

This guy back home had a dog named Jerry. Jerry would always run away and we'd hear this guy screaming for him at all hours of the night: "Jerry! Jerry!" He woke everybody up. It was very disturbing. More than a few times the screams of Jerry woke me up in the middle of the night, or worse, made a man's face pop into my head while I was jerking off into a dirty sock, making it take longer because I lost my concentration. But that's a different story all together. The point is naming a dog after a human is retarded, especially with all the really cool dog names out there although right God damn now I can't seem to think of one.

Steve and his canine boyfriend left and I was brought back to the present and my lame job and my dead ass and the fake kiss in my pocket and her, Ginger. She looked like a movie star so that's what I named her.

My eyes fixed on the door of the coffee shop, waiting for her to step back out into the world to help it make sense again. Five minutes passed, then ten. She hadn't come out. Maybe there was a back door that she exited without me knowing…a back door that she walked through and into the life of some other guy, changing it forever.

The breeze picked up and some of the air ran down the back of my sweater, running over my spine, bathing my bones. Everything just changed. Only slightly, but still, it changed. The noise from the street melted into the background, the smells from the restaurants flooded my nose and made my mouth water, and as I turned to my left, away from the coffee shop, I knew why. Jimmy was there. *King* was there. He stood like a giant in front of a humble sun and timid sky while I sat, squirmed, and stalked like a rodent. I think I forgot how beautiful he was.

"Hey, brother. How are you?"

How was I? Good question. I was sitting alone on a bench with a frozen ass. I was a peasant pining away for a queen that didn't know I existed. I had just gotten crushed in the gravity room. I had just witnessed a homosexual, man-dog peepshow and none of that mattered because in a few days I'd be dead and I'd be dead forever and nothing would be named after me. How was I? I'd say I was pretty damn shitty.

"I'm fine," I said. Like I mentioned before, it's a talent.

"You looked pretty upset when you left that magazine. Is everything all right?"

"I'm alright. How do you know, were you there?"

"And what about her? She's pretty, right?" he asked, avoiding my last question and motioning towards the coffee shop.

"Well, yeah. You saw her?"

"Yes, I saw her," he said as he took my bottle and drank nearly a quarter of it in one gulp. "But more importantly, I saw that you saw her. You've been staring over there for twenty minutes."

I chuckled with embarrassment and my face got hot. I took a drink.

"So what are you going to do? You going to ask her out or just spend the next few weeks wishing you did?"

I felt sick at the thought of having to ask her out. It was better to just not say anything and avoid being embarrassed as she laughed uncontrollably or being scalded as she threw her coffee in my face. Besides, why would I ask a girl out? Asking a girl out implies that you might want to create a romantic relationship or at least a friendship and for me those days are over. No more creation, only destruction.

Besides, I wanted to keep her in my mind as a fantasy that I could revisit any time over the next few days.

Champ! Yes! Champ was a good name for a dog.

As I entered the coffee shop, my legs shook from the lack of food and the excess of cigarettes and alcohol, combined with sick nerves. Jimmy sat on the bench, smiling wide. It took nearly ten minutes but he convinced me to ask her out. I always did what he said.

I saw her sitting by herself in the back of the room, sipping from a mug and reading a book with a black cover. I wanted to read books with black covers. They look super depressing.

She was alone amidst the lonely, just like me. I started walking up to her table. My lips were glued to my teeth. My heart was a jackhammer. I prayed for an earthquake or something to stop this from happening. I was a few feet away and she looked up. She looked right at me and I walked right past her and up to the counter. I was shaking.

"Can I help you?" the girl behind the counter asked.

Yeah, help me jam this cruller into my brain.

I rested against the counter, sweating and too freaked to turn around. I pretended to look at the different items I could buy but was really looking for something sharp to stab myself with.

"Um, okay, I'll have a, um…"

The girl behind the counter lost patience. "You know, this is a coffee shop. Did you realize that before you walked in?"

I killed her with my eyes.

"Really? I didn't know that. Thank you for enlightening me," I said, sarcastic as hell.

"No problem. It's *my pleasure* to serve all the psychopaths in town. Now, what would you like? Coffee?"

Oh! Even more sarcastic! I didn't need coffee. I was shaking as it was. "How about a tea? Do you have tea?"

"Yes. We have tea. How would you like it?"

"In a cup is fine."

She looked at me.

"Oh!" I yelled. "How would I *like* it….Surprise me." Oh man. I couldn't believe I'd said that.

"Okay, I'm thinking decaf for you."

While I stood in purgatory, ordering a surprise cup of tea, in order to pretend that I was there for tea and not to ask out Ginger, I noticed the face on the back of the milk carton behind the counter.

JOSE MARTINEZ	HEIGHT 3'6"
MISSING SINCE MAY 15TH	WEIGHT 61 LBS
AGE 8	

I was sad because I knew that Jose was dead. They'd probably never find the body either. That's all the parents want at this point anyway. Faced with the obvious, closure may be a consolation.

I lit up a cigarette.

"You can't smoke in here," the girl said.

I kept smoking. I faced away from Ginger breathing shallowly. I lifted my bottle out from inside my coat and downed some. I thought about walking out and telling Jimmy either that she turned me down or that she said she had a boyfriend, anything to get out of having to talk to her. I knew that he would know that I was lying. I didn't know how he'd know…he just would.

I took one deep breath and turned towards her table. She was gone. All that was left were a few dirty napkins. Relieved, I looked up and saw her floating out the door and into the gray. I put the napkins in my pocket and followed her. Out into the world she went and she went away. She was gone. So was Jimmy.

ALEX

I crawled up on the barstool. It felt like it was a mile high. I perched myself on top and put my bag between my legs, lit up a cigarette, and began drinking a shot of whiskey with a whiskey and Coke chaser. Then another shot of whiskey. The faces blurred. Another shot. The voices collided and shattered at my feet. Another shot. The cigarettes fed me. I lit one off the end of the last. I drank another shot. I tasted vomit. I took a sip of my whiskey and Coke. Pulled my cigarette. Took a drink. Did a shot. Pulled my cigarette. Took a drink. Took a piss. Pulled my cigarette. Tasted vomit. Laughed uncontrollably at nothing. Did a shot. Pulled my cigarette. Took a piss. Threw up in the sink. Threw up blood. Pulled my cigarette. Looked around. Saw the dead bodies. Pointed at all of them. Did a shot. Took a drink. Grabbed my bag and walked out.

I stumbled around until the beaten and covered sun finally relinquished power to the black. I laid down in an alley, clutched my bag and closed my eyes. *Am I alive or dead right now? What's the difference? Would I know either way?*

I jumped up, freezing. Where was I. What day was it? Tuesday, I thought.

I called Alex from a payphone. He invited me to his place. He asked me if I knew what time it was. I said I didn't have a watch. He told me it was four A.M. I took a cab.

"What the fuck happened to you?" he asked as he opened the door.

"I don't feel well. I think it's the flu."

"Yeah, well you fuckin' wreak like booze and shit. Come in… take a shower."

We kind of hugged each other as I walked by. I'd never been to his apartment. It was beautiful. Big Shot.

I turned the water up so hot it scalded me. I loved it. The steam enveloped me. I imagined it was poisonous gas and I breathed it in and held my breath. It burned my lungs. I scalded my back and arms with the water. I jerked off and came on the shower door. I started crying.

Alex and Andrea spent most of the morning talking kind of secretly, which is funny because from what Mom had told me they fought as much as anyone, ever. But there they were acting like two idiot spies who'd die before they'd divulge their secret information to anyone. Best friends all of a sudden. That's how some people are. They're enemies one day and best friends the next, as long as the new enemy is worse than the old one. When that enemy is gone it's back to hating the first one. Not that Andrea is like that, but Alex, he's a real big-shot prick sometimes and you could just tell that if he didn't get his way, he'd kick and scream about it. Anyway, I knew he didn't want me there. I'd leave soon. I just thought I should see him before…

"Perry, are you comfortable?"

"Yes."

He set me up in an extra bedroom. I was sitting on the bed wrapped in the blanket, staring out the window. The clock said 6:43. "I'm going to the airport," he said. "I'm leaving again on business. I'll be back in a few days. How long will you be staying?"

He wants me gone before that.

I didn't turn to face him. "Not long. I'll be gone before you get back."

"Okay. Well…it was nice seeing you. Take care of yourself."

"Thanks."

He closed the door. My eyes watered.

I got up and walked to the window. The shapes I traced in the mist that were born from my breath on the glass were coming alive and, I believe, plotting something big. So many people, I thought as I gazed out at all the lights in all the apartments of the adjacent buildings, so many people were on the streets, walking and pushing and rushing to get to work on time, unaware of me and my stare. If I had a gun I could kill all of them from up here. No matter. They are already dead. This whole city is one enormous mass grave.

I peeked out the door to make sure Alex was gone. I opened my backpack and took out the picture of all of us at his football game and thumbtacked it to the wall. I took out the other picture. I unfolded it. It upset me to see it but that was nothing new. The picture I drew was of Mom, when she didn't know I was watching. When Dad left for good and she was in the window, looking out and up, her emerald eyes sinking into a sea of saltwater. Her black curls spun out and away from her head, only moving when completely distraught, she'd run her hands through them. Tears ran over her bronze cheeks as her cheekbones pushed out against her skin and tears also ran down the sides of her perfectly pointed nose, falling off the tip and exploding beneath her. I drew her up close even though she was a good thirty feet away. I nearly went blind trying to focus. She cried for hours and I watched her all that time while I sat above her in the colossal oak tree on the left side of our house. To this day it's the only picture I've ever colored in. The colors…the colors just made it too real…and I've never loved things that are too real so I've stayed away from coloring since. I tacked the picture up and my mom stared back as I sat down on the bed. She looked like she was crying over me.

I put my head down on the pillow and it welcomed the little bit of energy I had left and asked me to stay awhile. It was nice. As I drifted away, I couldn't help but feel terribly alone and longed to be held by someone that loved me.

The last thing I remember as I fell into the black was a vision of a young man running across a field of pure, untouched snow. His footprints were the only scar across the massive white world. I couldn't for the life of me though, figure out if this was a memory of something I did when I was younger or just the first part of the dream, the part that happens while you're still awake.

FLOOD

I opened my eyes. My heart thumped up through my throat. Outside the window, the sky looked sad. Painted dark gray with some black, it was hard to tell if it was about to sleep or awaken. The clock on the nightstand said 7:14 and I couldn't tell if it was still morning or if I'd slept through and it was already nighttime.

The phone next to my head screamed like a scared child being chased by someone who liked to hurt things. Again, the phone, a screaming child. And again. My heart raced. I picked it up.

"Hello."

"Perry?"

"Hi Mom." My voice was a tired whisper.

"Perry, are you okay? You sound sick."

"I'm fine, it's just that, I just woke up," I said, still not knowing what day I had woken up in. "I didn't think I'd hear from you."

"Perry, I've been worried about you."

Mom always made me miss being home and being with her and that was the last thing I needed right then. I could not let any feelings for her stop me from what I had to do.

I am a lit fuse.

"I'm sorry, but I'm okay."

There was silence for a long second.

"So, you've been taking care of yourself?"

"Yeah, kind of," I lied.

I am a horrible secret.

"Perry I really wish you'd come home."

Her words traveled through me, into my ear and down my

throat, and further down into my heart, and breaking off in my stomach. My eyes got wet and I pushed out a few barely audible words.

"I can't, Mom...there's just nothing there for me."

"Perry, I love you. Please be well."

I dropped the phone down to my side and slid it into the base, hanging it up.

"I love you, too," I said. "I love you, too."

I sat Indian style on my bed and rummaged through my bag looking for the sketchpad I'd been neglecting. The lightning lit up the now dark-black sky as if the sun had sneaked into the moon's yard and left before anyone realized it. A thunder ball shook the world, sounding off, letting us know it needed to be heard and that it was not to be outdone. It'd been cold, bleak, and rainy for three days.

I sat in front of the mirror and looked at my face. I could see all the oil and dirt actually forming pimples. I could see microscopic organisms crawling along my eyelids, brows, and lips, eating me alive.

I am a hideous creature.

I started to draw myself. At one hundred miles an hour I furiously stroked back and forth with my pencil. Each line a mini-declaration of self-loathing. I drew myself as a monster, hating and proving that hate by stabbing myself to death each time the pencil hit the paper. Slicing my face open, I made my eyes black and my teeth broken. My lips were worms and my ears spiders...

The phone rang, interrupting the misery that spewed from my pencil. It rang four times. The machine picked up. The person hung up before it beeped. I drew blood and bruises. The phone rang again. I drew scabs and slices. It rang again. I jammed the pencil down, point first, through my face, tearing the paper. It rang again. I answered it.

"Hello."

"Perry," the voice said, sure it was me.

"Jimmy? How did you get this number?"

"Hey, meet me outside your place in fifteen minutes and dress nice."

"What? Where are you? Where are we going?"

"I can't tell you. Be downstairs in, well now it's fourteen and a half minutes."

"I can't. I mean, I'm in the middle of something," I said, fighting back the urge to scream *Yes! Yes! I will come! I'll be down in fourteen and a half minutes! Yes, fourteen and a half minutes until I get to hang out with you! Fourteen and a half minutes!*

"Perry, listen, that girl, the one we saw today? Her and her friends are at a bar on Fourteenth Street. We're going to go see them. Come downstairs."

He hung up.

I pulled hard on a borrowed cigarette and asked him how he got my brother's number.

"Your name is Perry Patton right? You told me you had a brother named Alex. It's not rocket science."

He had a bottle of red wine in his coat and we passed it back and forth as we walked through the video game. I was wearing my nicest blue sweater and black pants. Jimmy looked like a model from a magazine. His jaw was frozen, carved, creating a profile that silhouetted perfectly against the buildings. He was like them. Like the buildings. Built like them, strong like them. Not weak and fragile like me and everyone. He was made of steel, immoveable.

We arrived at the bar. A line of about twenty people stood out front, looking plastic. Jimmy walked right up to the front of the line, with me a few steps behind. Jimmy did whatever he wanted. I loved it. Everyone turned and stared at us. I felt like a movie star. He whispered something to the orangutan out front and in an instant we were in. I turned and looked through the glass at the people on the outside who longed to be where we were now. The girls were half dressed and shivering, their hair being blown around, undoing all the work they had done before they came out, slowly revealing the *real* them. Making them nervous because they don't think that guys want to know the *real* them, only the illusion. Once you know how the magician does the trick, it's no longer fun to watch him do it. And the guys, with cologne smells fading and pumped muscles beneath tight, sleeveless shirts that revealed one ridiculous tribal tattoo after the next.

These are The Dolls. They will die to belong. Yet, the name-brand clothes and the commercial they'd become while wearing them did nothing to get them to where I was. I was better than them. All of us were. All of us on the inside. And we all knew it.

"Hey, Perry, how are you?"

Smoke had never spoken to me like that. It wasn't like she was *happy* to see me, but more like she wasn't *unhappy* to see me.

"I'm fine. I mean, I'm great," I replied, trying to show her what she was missing. Yeah, I told her I was great. That showed her.

Ocean was there also. I saw him talking to some beautiful girl against the bar, close enough to kiss her. The second he saw me, however, he pulled back and made a beeline over to me.

"Perry, what the fuck is up?" Ocean asked, giving me that cool handshake hug that guys give to other guys to show the people watching that they *really* like each other.

"Nothing…is up."

"You need a cocktail?"

Ocean and I had barely said hello the other night. I puked up some coke in front of him and was embarrassed as hell about it but I guess he likes people that do that because he seemed excited to see me.

"Yeah, whiskey, rocks, please."

Dirtmouth was there, too. He had seen the guys at happy hour and tagged along. He hugged me, softly, like he didn't want to hurt me. It was kind of weird.

Jimmy smiled when I ordered. "Give me a red. Me and my brother Perry are drinking tonight."

We all slammed our drinks, pulled our cigarettes, and got lost inside the music. The energy surrounded us. We had it. Whatever *it* was. We had it. Everyone felt it. People gathered around us, trying to join our party. Some made their way in and others were cast aside. But through it all, I was always kept close. Always kept in the circle. It was King, Smoke, Ocean, Dirtmouth, and me. Just the five of us. A team. A crew. Whatever. We were together for the first time since I blew my first line in the nowhere room. Only now I was an equal and not the new guy puking in the corner.

"Hey, do a shot, mother fucker!" Ocean screamed, grabbing me around the neck with a huge hand and putting a shot of what smelt like hot puke in my face. Hot puke, a.k.a. tequila. We'd already done four or five shots of it. Ocean grabbed me the way you'd grab your little brother you hadn't seen in a while but loved more than anything. Alex never grabbed me like that. Jimmy just stared and smiled. He didn't drink shots, just red wine and sometimes whiskey.

I was there with my new friends. They liked me. They accepted me. Being around them, it made me less freaked about everything. Like an astronaut, hurtling through space, not afraid of anything. I was outside myself. Outside myself and in the center of the action, not looking in, longing to be.

I'd never belonged anywhere in my whole life. I felt bad that I'd be leaving soon.

The fun ended as quickly as it began when some pour soul knocked into Ocean and spilled his drink on him. All the guy had to do was say he was sorry. I think that's all that Ocean wanted.

"Hey, you don't say excuse me!" Ocean screeched at the guy, who was pretty damned big himself. Much bigger than me. Not as big as Ocean, but still pretty big.

"Excuse me for what? It's a fucking bar," he replied through his teeth as he turned towards us and put his arms up in an almost taunting manner. "It's crowded. Get over it!"

Ocean started to move towards him. The guy, who I named Burner because of the blonde and red streaks in the front of his hair that looked a little like fire and a lot like ridiculous, wasn't backing down. He must've been real drunk. A bunch of Big Shots tried to get in between them, saying things like, "Okay, we don't need any trouble here. Let's just forget about it." *I hate Big Shots.*

In an instant they were tossed aside as Ocean rushed at Burner, clocking him across the jaw with a monster's fist. My ears hurt from the sound it made. Burner fell backwards into that same group of Big Shots, causing their drinks to spill everywhere and hopefully blinding them all. Then Ocean blew through and kicked the already reeling Burner in the face. His nose exploded.

I got sick from the sight of it. I'd never been in a fight before. I was freaked seeing it up close. My heart raced and my palms were soaked as I stood on the outskirts of the circle that had formed around them. I let the swaying crowd push me around like an empty bottle in rough surf. Also, I was thinking about how good it feels to be inside a circle and how numb it feels not to be.

The bouncers responded. Three of them held Ocean down as two more helped Burner to his feet. His face was bashed apart. There was blood everywhere. He cried like a child. *Dumb fuck should have just said sorry.*

Ocean writhed and kicked and screamed as he was dragged out the door by all five bouncers. He was such a fuckin' maniac. I loved it.

I got caught up in the fray, being pushed and pulled towards the door by a spinning crowd all wanting to be part of the action. They all wanted to be able to tell their friends that they saw what happened, to recount all the events like bar room newscasters. It seems that inside the madness, everyone is still looking for something that they can carry as a trophy, whether it is some sweet pussy's phone number, the amount of shots they just did while you went to the bathroom, or all the details involving a guy named Burner being buried at the bottom of the Ocean, washed away.

We fell out onto the street. It was pouring, raining like it had never rained before, like it was trying something new. I saw lightning carve an electric zig-zag tattoo into the sky's heart. I wished it hit me. I wanted to feel its energy. I wanted it to burn my soul out through my skin.

I am a lightning rod.

Ocean was still amped up, screaming and spitting on the windows of the place. The bouncers stood guard at the door,

I think a little afraid. I was drunk as hell, laughing and getting wet, traveling back in time with each raindrop that blessed me by ending its long journey on my head or shoulders. Raindrops, the tears from the sky's eyes, hurtling toward earth, stopped only a few feet from the ground where they were destined to land, because I was standing there. It made me sad because I was the reason their journey was unfinished. They never got to where they were supposed to. Something stopped them and they never made it all the way. I guess that's the way it is sometimes.

By now half the bar had piled out onto the street, screaming and dancing about in the downpour. It was right then that I realized that I hadn't seen Jimmy in a while. I hadn't seen him since before the fight started. Yeah, he'd been gone that long. I wondered where he was. Was he talking to Ginger somewhere? Somewhere private? Away from me? He said she was going to be there but I hadn't seen her. Fuck him if he is. Fuck both of them.

Just then, Smoke, who seemed to be much less wet than everyone else, grabbed me by my hand and pulled me into the crowd that was walking with the same legs to somewhere else, somewhere away from there. She pulled me against a building, under an awning. She opened a tiny cellophane bag filled with sugar. She put the end of a key inside and scooped some onto it. She put it up to my nose and I inhaled it through my left nostril. It burned a bit. I gagged. She did one.

"A quick blast," she said.

The back of my throat became numb. I felt kind of awake.

I asked her for another blast. We both did one more.

I asked Smoke if she had seen Jimmy. When the last time she had seen him was. Was he talking to some girl? None of her answers satisfied me.

He was gone.

Our pants were soaked from the bottom to just under the knee from walking through puddles of once-pure water now being polluted by this filthy city street. In every puddle, faces appeared and dissolved before I could kneel down and fully see them: Mom, Dad, Alex, there for an instant and then gone forever.

Ocean raged. He ripped his shirt off and pulled it through one of the belt loops in his pants, securing it. It was freezing and raining but he didn't care. He only had a white tank top on and within five seconds it was drenched and stuck to him.

It was the first time I had ever seen him with his shirt off. His back was as big as a billboard and I could see that he had a tattoo that covered the entire thing. On it, I could barely make out through the rain, the shape of a person and what looked like unfinished, kind of messy work in the background.

"*Whoooo hooooo* mother fucker!" he screamed. "Let's get this fucker started. It's only eleven thirty."

Ocean had a fan club at this point, a group of seven or eight leeches who had clung to him when we were swept up in the flood, after the fight, after Burner got soaked.

Smoke called them hipsters. "They're all transplants from other cities whose fathers own car dealerships or whatever. They come here on Daddy's dime and act as if they've been living here their whole lives."

They were wearing tight jeans and button-down shirts with oversized collars. They looked like they were in a band, or at least thought they were. Some of them wore big black-rimmed glasses and had cool spiked hair. I was sure that none of them were as smart as I was. Or as talented. I was convinced of it. Fuck 'em.

So you had the Hipsters who I just described. The Big Shots

who were the suit-wearing, deal-making types. The Dolls who were the walking commercials who'd die to belong, and the Sick Fucks who referred to just about everybody else. That's it. That's everyone. I categorized the shit out of all those people. I had names for all of them. Well, except for me and my friends. I didn't have a name for us yet. The one thing I did know is that we were all dying to kill ourselves.

"Give me a hot dog, bitch," Ocean yelped at one of those guys that sell them on the street, off of a cart. He was soaked, the hot dog vendor, hiding beneath an umbrella that was severely overmatched. I guess he waited outside the bars to catch the hungry drunks before they went home to burp, fart, and masturbate. He looked undersized, shaking in the face of a tidal wave.

"Well c'mon! Give me a fucking dog, you dildo immigrant fuck! I'm starving."

"Dollar seventy-five," he said, barely standing his ground.

"What'dya say, you chink fuck!?"

I didn't think the guy was Chinese. He looked more Filipino. I did a report on the Philippines when I was in tenth grade.

"Shouldn't you be somewhere singing karaoke! All you gooks love that shit! Right?"

The hipsters were laughing.

"Dollar seventy-five," he said, raising his voice and speaking right into a monster's mouth.

Bad things were about to happen. Ocean was on fire. His shirt was still off and the freezing rain slammed down on all of us. His whole entourage stood and watched him harass a tiny, freezing little man, who was risking his life for a dollar seventy-five. Everyone was laughing their asses off. Except me and Smoke.

I couldn't watch anymore. I needed to say something. The

little man, who I named Battleship for his ability to stay afloat amidst a crashing Ocean, was running out of time before he'd get buried beneath the waves. But just as my voice was rising from my chest, something incredible happened. Ocean, who by now was inches from Battleship, sharing his breath, reached into his back pocket and pulled out his wallet. He opened it, revealing a garden of green. He took out two singles.

"With sauerkraut," he whispered, handing the money to Battleship. "I like you man. You got heart."

As we walked, soaked, through a world slowly falling underwater I watched a calm Ocean with caution. He seemed sedate as he held the hot dog close, not eating it yet. But with Ocean, you had to be careful. Things could change in an instant. It could get pretty scary.

In front of me, standing under a green awning in front of the next bar, talking on a cell phone, trying to hide from the rain being thrown about by demons and monsters, stood a drenched Ginger. She shivered with her jacket over her wet head. Her hair looked darker wet than the soft blonde color it was the day before. The day she stole me away. She was alone. I walked up within ten feet of her and stopped, staring, uncaring. She was beautiful and I needed something beautiful in my life. So what if she didn't reciprocate? I couldn't be disappointed if she wasn't *the girl*, the one who lives in the future killing herself on her way back to me. When you're hopeless you can't be disappointed.

"Hi," I said.

She barely looked up. She turned her whole body away from me and continued her conversation. I hate cell phones and I hate people that use cell phones. Everybody's so damned important.

"Oh God. This thing is disgusting!" Ocean screamed, spitting a gnarled piece of hot dog and bun into a flowing river. The piece bobbed up and down, barely staying above water as it rushed past me, like a little man gone overboard in a ship. It had no chance. Then he cocked his arm back and launched the rest of it up over the chain-link fence that prevented all but the most agile from entering the alley. As it reached its peak, the hot dog separated from the bun and continued its flight upward as the bun split in two at the crease and fell away, two separate ways. It reminded me of when astronauts who aren't afraid of anything fly a rocket ship up tearing the sky in half on their way to outer space. And right when they get far enough up that the rocket can survive on its own, it drops the boosters that helped get it there. They fall to the earth as the rocket begins its voyage. But without those boosters that get tossed aside, the rocket would never be able to get to the point that it gets to where it no longer needs them. It's like my life. I needed certain things to help me get to a certain place, a place where I decided that I no longer needed those things. So those things that got me there got tossed aside, things like algebra or my family. Now I can make up my mind for myself. There's nothing wrong with that. It's just what so.

"Okay, so I'll see you in a little bit. Hurry," Ginger said to whoever was inside her phone. She looked up at me: her eyes, bright green cat's eyes. They struck me hard, picking up the neon in the sign behind her. Every time she blinked, it was as if someone was turning two tiny televisions on and off. She smiled. She stood still.

She burns like fire, playing tricks on my eyes. Changing shape and color but still keeping me back because I am afraid to get burned.

By this point the crowd had stretched long and thin like a snake in front of the door. Ocean pushed everyone aside and forced his way to the front. Ginger grabbed me by the arm, nearly piercing my skin with her nails. She was freezing. Not like fire at all. I felt her through her jacket and she was freezing. We followed in Ocean's wake. He still had his shirt off and for the first time, with him directly in front of me, I could see somewhat clearly the tattoo that draped his back. The painted picture shook me. It made my stomach fall away. I couldn't fuckin' believe what I was seeing. There, through the rain and the alcohol and the coke, I saw the person on his skin, sitting Indian-style on the floor in front of some messy, unfinished work.

It was me.

Shadow Man

We fell through the door and Ocean was gone. I reached out for him, my fingers scraping at the face in the tattoo. *My face.* It disappeared.

Blowing through the faceless swarm, we arrived at the bar, drunk and wet and spinning. Ginger pulled me close. Her friends were there but I didn't care. I stared at everybody that all looked exactly the same, trying to see where Ocean settled. Before I knew it, I had a beer in my left hand and was doing a shot of something clear and burning with my right.

With my mouth drenched and reeling from the poison and my head spinning from Ocean's tattoo, Ginger pulled up close and kissed me. She bit my bottom lip softly and pulled it down towards her. She let me go and we stood staring at each other for a moment. Ocean was forgotten.

I felt my face and neck turning red. I bent down to kiss her back, but just when I was a few inches away, right at the point where there was no turning back, when I couldn't even pretend I was trying to tell her a secret or anything, she turned away, distracted by her girlfriend pointing at something or someone on the other side of the bar.

"I'll be right back," she said, and vanished.

I reached out and grabbed a small stirring straw off the bar and began chewing it. It tasted exactly like nothing.

Jimmy sneaked up and slapped me on the back.

"C'mon. Let's go," he said, walking towards the back of the bar.

"Where you going? Where the fuck have you been? There was a fight at the other bar. He—"

"I had to take care of some shit."

"Yeah, but he wrecked this guy. It was so sick…"

"Perry, look…he, well, maybe he's not the best person for you to be hangin' out with."

"I thought you guys were tight."

He laughed. "We are, it's just that his life, well, it can get a little scary sometimes. And that's fine for him. But for you, well, you may get inside of his world and not like what you find. I'm just trying to look out for you. That's all."

He pushed open the bathroom door and made sure no one was inside. We stepped in and he closed the door behind us and leaned against it so no one could come in. He pulled out a bag of sugar and poured some on his hand. Right on the skin along the bone that attaches the thumb to the wrist, in the little pocket that forms there when you flex it. He snorted hard. Someone pushed on the door and his hand shook a bit. They started banging on the door. He gave me some…a lot. I blew it up. I gagged and dry heaved.

"Check my nose, brother," he said, leaning his head back for me to see if he had any coke in his nostrils.

"You're good. Me?"

"Beautiful."

As he took his weight off the door, a bouncer pushed his way in, slamming the door wide open and into the sink. He saw Jimmy. He saw King. He didn't say anything other than a few calming words to the line of Dolls, Hipsters, and Big Shots that were waiting to piss.

The music blew a hole in my head. The lights killed me alive. The coke shot lightning into my blood. Jimmy disappeared.

Ginger was on the other side of the bar. She was talking to a man wearing a black baseball cap with a hooded black sweatshirt over it with long sleeves nearly covering both his hands. I got glimpses of his face. It was dark. The darkness always freaks me. He had facial hair like he hadn't shaved in a week. He had no definitive features—no eyes, no mouth, no nose. The shadows from the hood and cap covered him. He only existed as a dark hallway, a lightless room, a black night. He was Shadow Man.

They spoke closely. Shadow Man held her tight and spoke right into her face. They were arguing. I breathed shallowly. I hadn't realized how crowded it was in there. People bumped me, constantly. I turned away from Ginger and Shadow Man. They were arguing hard and violently. My hands were sweating. I felt tense and jittery. My skin itched. I wanted to tear it off so my blood could melt down through the cracks in the floor. My knees were made of jelly but not a delicious kind. My heart was coming through my ribcage, pushing its way out of my chest. I thought it would stop at any moment.

I started to make my way to the door. I needed air. I felt a hand on my shoulder and was spun around like a top. I was staring into Ocean's face.

"Whose that fuckin' guy talking to your girl?"

"I don't know," I replied, a bit freaked but also a little excited that he called Ginger, *my girl.*

"C'mon, let's go have a talk with him."

"No. It's alright. I'm sure it's nothing."

Jimmy showed up.

"C'mon P.," Ocean said, giving me the first nickname I'd had since I was fourteen and everyone called me Throw Up after I puked up hot dogs at the fair back home. "You gotta show that guy that you're not to be fucked with."

"Hey, maybe Perry's had enough excitement for tonight. Maybe it's time to go home," Jimmy said.

Ocean got close to Jimmy. He dwarfed him.

"Maybe you should go home. Perry is just fine hanging out with me," he said in a horrible raspy whisper that made my stomach turn.

Jimmy didn't flinch.

"C'mon," he said, pulling my arm. I almost fell down he was so strong. I turned back and Jimmy was watching us. I saw Ginger and Shadow Man on the other side of the bar. They were still arguing. He was inches from her face with his right hand digging into her left shoulder.

"You gotta do something about that," Ocean said.

My stomach wrenched. I felt like I was going to shit my pants.

"No…I…I, can't. I've never been in a fight before."

I felt tiny.

Ocean turned away in disgust and started walking down our side of the bar. People jumped out of his way. He was enormous. I was a few feet behind him. I had completely forgotten about the man on his back until I saw him staring at me. I saw me staring at me. As we got to the end of the bar he swung out wide, making a huge left turn and heading back towards Ginger and Shadow Man. I followed in his footsteps. He reached out as he passed the vacant pool table and with his right hand grabbed a pool stick off of it. We were coming up on them. I knew what he was going to do. I couldn't stop it. No one could. As we got about ten feet away, he flipped the cue upside down in his hand so that he was *holding* the thin end and the thick end was pointing up.

I could see them, Ginger with her back to us and Shadow Man, whose face I still couldn't make out, standing on top of her, towering.

I took a deep breath and held it. I wanted to scream before it happened.

Ocean wound up as we came upon them and swung the pool cue, like a baseball bat, over the top of Ginger's head, striking Shadow Man in the temple. The cue shook and rattled in his hands. It shattered everywhere.

Shadow Man fell. He was a tree chopped down amidst a crowded forest. He disappeared and new faces took his place. It was almost like he was never there. I couldn't swallow. Vomit shot up my esophagus. My mouth was dead hair and cotton.

Time sped up with the help of a screaming jukebox. Shadow Man was down, writhing and maybe dying while Ocean reached for me while I reached for Ginger.

The vultures were circling. People whispered. Only a few Sick Fucks saw what happened and most of them were probably scared to death. But they whispered, whispered to people who whispered to other people who looked up and then whispered to other people. Pretty soon I knew we would be swallowed, whole.

Ginger was down on her knees at Shadow Man's side as he laid bathing in his own blood. Down on her knees almost praying. For what, I didn't know. I had a soft hand on her shoulder, not wanting to disturb her in case this pile was her love, and her talking to me in the first place is what got him there. To the wet floor of a cold bar that didn't matter to anyone, anywhere.

Ocean's breath burned my ear. "Let's get the fuck outta here man."

I bent down. My chest pounded. "Let's go," I said to Ginger.

She looked up at me and the way the light hit her face, I swear I saw her bones through her skin. I saw her the way the universe will know her forever. She was a skeleton wearing thin, poorly fitting clothing. She had no hope, just like everybody else.

She reached into Shadow Man's coat pocket and pulled out a huge bag of sugar. She grabbed my hand and I pulled her through a circling pack of vultures and away from a shadow that had nothing to follow anymore.

It was nearly three A.M. Ocean was silent. Ginger held my arm, pulling herself close. The rain had stopped. Jimmy was gone. The flood was over.

As we walked past the front of the bar, I saw Smoke talking to some guy in the corner. Some guy that was just like me the night she and I first met. Some guy who was sucking down smoke, coughing with watering eyes, all the while falling in love with loneliness and misery. He had no idea what he was in for.

"Hey, what's your name?" Ginger asked.

"Perry. Perry Patton."

Her phone rang as I spoke and she turned away from me as she answered it.

"I know. Alright. A half hour," she said, and hung up.

"I've gotta go," she said, smiling at me. "Meet me over at Cherry Bar tomorrow at ten Perry, Perry Patton."

She kissed me on the mouth and pulled away while I was still kissing, leaving me alone and frozen in the middle of the wet street.

She disappeared.

Ocean walked me to Alex's. His shirt was still off, soaked from the flood earlier. We walked side by side with me twisting my neck around every few steps to see the tattoo on his back.

We didn't say a word about what happened. About Battleship, Shadow Man, Ginger, or Jimmy. We just flowed slowly down the street, more tired than drunk, but still quite aware of each other as the new day blew a hole in the night.

Snow

My dreams tasted like sugar and steel. They invited me to dance with the dead. Ghosts and spirits shot around me as I walked through a warehouse where bodies hung from meat hooks. Every face on every body was mine.

I pulled the shades and was rewarded with a cold, bleak sky as I rose just briefly and then collapsed back into the bed that stunk like garlic and decay.

What day was it? Thursday?

My head was heavy and someone was hammering inside it. I felt the weight and the worry of the dying inside of me. Images of people working out on complicated machines, trying to trim their fat asses, bounced across the television set as I rolled back and forth, burning. The clock said 5:16.

I looked at the picture of me and the family and smiled. Then I looked at the picture of Mom and stopped smiling. In fact, I nearly fell out of the bed because of what I saw. The picture I'd drawn of Mom years earlier, that I'd looked at five-hundred times since, was different. I reached out and touched it; it was the same paper. The spacing and style were the same, all Mom's features were the same, except this time on this picture, her eyes, which had always been bright and wide open, were closed.

The buzzer in the apartment shrieked. I stuck my head out from my room. Andrea answered it.

"Yes?"

"Hey is Perry there?"

It was Ocean.

"Yes…uh, who should I say is calling?"

I started walking towards the door.

"Just tell him to come downstairs so we can smoke a joint…"

I jumped in front of Andrea and hit the button so his voice cut off. I smiled at her and shrugged my shoulders.

"Uh, I'll be down in a minute man," I said and smiled at her again and then nodded a few times. And then, for some psychotic reason, I started whistling. Like *whistling* makes anyone look innocent.

Down on the street I hugged the buildings, trying my best to stay out of the rain's way. My underwear was dirty, my socks were dirty, my face and ass and teeth and ears were dirty, and I didn't care one bit.

We passed a joint back and forth while we walked. Nobody cared. It totally burned my throat. I imagined the skin on my throat peeling off and sliding down into my stomach to be digested along with the alcohol and the lining of my belly.

I am a cannibal.

We sat under an awning in front of a deli and finished the joint. He bought two iced teas and mixed them with whiskey and we drank and watched the rain. I hadn't asked him about the tattoo on his back yet.

"Hey, you see that mailbox?" Ocean asked, pointing at the blue beast standing guard on the corner.

"Yep."

"Betcha your first drink tonight that for as long as we sit here, not one person mails a letter and doesn't check to make sure it went down."

"Yeah?"

"You know. They mail their letter and...wait, here comes someone now."

A man with no face, well no face worth speaking of, walked up. "You see. He opens the slot. He puts the letter in..."

His voice got louder, more excited.

"...he closes it. C'mon asshole, check it out. Wouldn't want to lose that letter you're sending to the penis enlargement headquarters in France."

No Face paused for a moment and then...

"And there he goes!" Ocean screamed. "He opens the slot again and checks to see if the letter is gone. Whooo hoooo!!! We have a winner! Perry, tell him what he's won!"

"Two tickets to watch me get drunk off my ass and puke on my shirt!"

We died laughing. No Face heard us. *Fuck him.*

"People are so predictable," Ocean said.

Not me. Nobody could predict all the different ways I'd try to destroy myself.

I pulled hard on my cigarette, took a drink, and asked, "Hey what's up with your tattoo?"

"I thought you'd ask about that, P..."

"Yeah?"

"Yeah, everybody does," he said, pointing to the one on his neck that said *love life* in clean, skinny, black writing. His eyes were bloodshot from the weed. "I guess it could mean a lot of things but for me it means livin' it up. Doing every single thing as hard as I can."

"Yeah?"

He stood up and walked out into the rain. He grabbed an empty wooden box off a garbage pile on the curb and flipped it over. He threw it down right in the middle of the racing crowd.

He stood on top of it. "Yeah Perry," he said really loud, like he was giving a speech. Some people stopped, but most ignored him or at least tried to. "That's why I drink all the drinks, Perry. It's why I snort all the drugs. Why I fight all the fights and why I fuck all the girls!" he hollered from well over eight feet high. "That's why I destroy anything even remotely boring or tedious. That's why I will never get married. It's why I'll spit whiskey on this asshole," he said as he sipped and then spit some of his drink out from between his teeth, right into some Big Shot's face. The guy was totally humiliated but kept walking because Ocean was a maniac. "That's why I'll jerk off all over this lady's face," he said miming the international jerk-off motion right into some Doll bitch's face as she walked by. "And that's why I should be your next mayor."

He jumped down. We both laughed our asses off.

"C'mon let's go," he said.

I slammed the rest of my whiskey-iced tea.

"You know, you owe me my first drink tonight, P. Every single person has checked to see if their letters have gone down."

His mood changed. He said it kind of pissed off. But he was right: everyone had checked.

He struck a match and lit a cigarette and with the still-burning match, he lit the rest of the book on fire. He walked over to the mailbox and dropped it inside. He checked to make sure it went down.

Friday night never felt like that before. I was numb, exhausted, and still a little high from the weed. I felt more self-destructive than ever and couldn't wait to crawl inside a tall glass of whiskey and drown myself. It was 8:30 and Andrea was at dinner. She left me a note.

Perry,
Went to dinner.
Blah, blah, blah. Take care of yourself. Blah, blah, blah.
Love, Andrea

I shaved with an old, dull razor and now I wore a bleeding mask. The radio was telling me everything I needed to hear as I got ready to meet Ocean downstairs and Ginger at Cherry Bar. The final touches of hair gel and blood cleanup did nothing to make me feel any more attractive. In fact, I was certain I was getting uglier. I was a little uglier than I was the day before. The day before I was a little uglier than the day before that and the next day would be more of the same. I was sliding and I could not stop and I loved every minute of it.

The cigarettes gave me life. I was a sick, nicotine-sucking mosquito buzzing through the room who needed to be swatted against the wall. I took a swig of whiskey.

I am Jack Daniels' long lost nephew.

Some big shot was on the television. "We are a country of addicts, Joan. In fact, addiction is part of the human condition," he said. "And I'm not only talking about alcohol and drugs. Sure that's what everyone thinks when you say addiction, but you've got coffee and cigarettes…"

I took a drag and looked over at the picture of Mom. Her eyes were back open.

"And what about things like television? Do you know how many people are addicted to television? People can be addicted to anything. They are addicted to pornography and masturbating, exercising and working. Do you know how many people each year work themselves to death?"

I hoped Andrea's boss wasn't watching this. He *should* work himself to death.

"...sex, celebrity, speed, hair dye, nasal spray, dental floss, skydiving...these are all the new addictions. People are addicted to being right, to getting attention, to having their voices heard."

Big Shots.

"Wars last for generations because people are addicted to suffering and misery and anger. They wouldn't know what to do without it. Everyone is addicted. I mean, even the monk in the temple who rises at four-thirty A.M. and meditates for ten hours a day, who eats only a little rice and some miso soup all day long, he's addicted to the high he gets in the meditative state. I bet you cannot find one person in this country and maybe the world who isn't addicted to something. We need to face it, Joan. Addiction is no longer a bad word."

I am a big fat motherfuckin' addict.

"You talk to Jimmy tonight?" I asked Ocean, breaking the silence that had swallowed us in the five minutes since he'd met me in front of the apartment.

I thought, as the words fell out, that maybe that wasn't the best question to ask, since they were pretty heated the night before and seeing as how he was a fuckin' maniac...but I said *fuck it.* I do Big Shot stuff like that sometimes.

"No," he said, exhaling cigarette smoke.

He was such a fuckin' mental patient. Four hours earlier, he was my best friend and now he was acting like I was some annoying little tag-a-long.

"You guys don't talk every day?"

"We talk every day, just not today," he said, looking straight ahead.

"You pissed at him or something?"

I'm funny because this guy, he was insane. I knew that. I had seen him kick Burner, a guy twice *my* size, in the face so hard that his nose turned from solid to liquid. Then he smashed Shadow Man across the temple with a pool cue, maybe killing him, and never said a word about either of them. And earlier that day he'd lit an entire mailbox on fire. People's letters and bills and whatever, torched.

"So what's the deal with you guys? Did ya go to school together or something?"

"What's with all the questions?"

"Just curious. I mean you guys seem like you know each other pretty well, that's all."

"Yeah well, things aren't always what they seem. Sometimes the people that act like they're your friends are the ones that smile wide while watching you die. He and I have a relationship, yeah. But I wouldn't say we're friends. So drop it."

We walked into the bar and everyone stopped for a second and stared at us, then continued taking up space. I didn't care. I was with Ocean. No one would dare say a word to us; if they did, they'd find out what it meant to suffer.

He lit up a cigarette and ordered two beers. I pounded my beer in under a minute and ordered two more. I lit a cigarette and nearly inhaled the whole thing on my first drag. I acted calm as hell when he asked if I saw her anywhere.

"Who? Oh yeah, her. Nah. I don't care either. I just felt like coming out. I didn't come to see her. In fact, I kind of forgot she was coming."

"Right," he replied, like a condescending fuck.

I was full of shit but was still trying to play it cool. I stood against the bar, leaning on my elbows and watching in the mirror everybody that all looked exactly the same, hoping to catch a glimpse of her—a comet on a cloudy night.

"Well, don't look now, but that girl you *didn't* come to see is walking up behind you," Ocean said.

I spun around and knocked over two empty glasses that had been left behind by two Big Shots, probably out celebrating their first hard-ons. The glass shattered at her feet as she followed her big green eyes out of the darkness.

"Oh man, I'm sorry!" I yelled at the top of my lungs. "How are you?!" again at the top of my lungs like a circus ringmaster, cutting through the silence that always follows the sound of broken glass.

"I'm fine," she whispered, stepping around the debris and kissing me on the cheek. She squeezed between us and up to the bar. "Have you been waiting long?"

"No, in fact Perry forgot that you were going to be here," Ocean said laughing.

"No I didn't," I said, trying to hide my red face by turning away, pretending that something caught my attention.

"Let me buy you another beer," she said.

I switched to whiskey. I sipped and nearly gagged on my drink watching her wash away beneath the weight of whatever she was trying to run from. Something happened with Shadow Man the night before. Maybe she'd dated him. Maybe she'd owed him something. Money was my first thought, but it could've been anything. There are lots of things you can owe to people; money is just one of them. And now she was drinking, smoking, and holding my hand like we were in love and had been forever. She was running a million miles an hour, standing still.

"Don't you want to know who he is?"

She was talking about Shadow man. The guy Ocean may have killed the night before. I did want to know who he was, and if he knew who I was, and if he wanted me deader than I wanted myself.

"Yes."

"He is someone that has been giving me trouble. Someone I should never have gotten involved with. Thank you for what you did last night."

"Me? I didn't do…"

"I know it was you who saved me. You may not have swung the stick, but you are the reason why it was swung, so thank you," she said, putting her index finger over my lips, shushing me as I tried to speak.

Hours passed. I was on my sixth whiskey. Ginger and I were talking close and sometimes kissing softly.

I am the feeling that nothing can stop me. I am powerful. I am a killing spree.

Ocean was at the end of the bar, talking to some girl with long, black hair and pale skin. He was probably telling her about mailboxes. I wanted to ask him about the tattoo on his back. I leaned down to tell Ginger I was going when she asked me to hold her cigarette while she rummaged through her bag.

Looking around, I noticed that nearly everyone in there was smoking—people with burning cigarettes in dirty mouths and virgin cigarettes behind big ears, with cigarettes smoking in ashtrays and drowning at the bottom of glasses, and being crushed beneath heavy feet on the cold floor. Smoke rose from the mouth of nearly every person in every group of people in the place. Hot, white smoke painted our faces. It stuck to us, to me. It was our ritual, our meditation.

"Oww!!!" I screamed as the cigarette that had nearly burned away bit my finger with a mouth of fire. I dropped it as everyone within earshot turned to find me sucking on my finger and dancing around on my tiptoes in an oddly homosexual pain ritual. Ginger laughed with freshly painted lips. She pulled me close.

"Hey Perry, I want you to meet someone," Ocean said, sneaking up from behind me. "This is…"

I knew who she was. She was the girl with the long, black hair and pale skin he had been talking to for the last hour. Pale white, like snow. She was pretty up close. Her eyes were like glass. I could see right through them. I could see into her and I could tell that just like me, she didn't believe in anything or belong anywhere. She was sad and she was inside of me.

"Hi, nice to meet you," I said, pulling slightly away from Ginger and sticking my hand out to shake hers. The touch of her hand made me numb, just like snow. The pain in my burned finger was gone. I felt like I was going to cry. I wanted to kiss her. Hold her. Die with her.

"We're going to the bathroom. Wait here," Ginger said to me, grabbing Snow by the arm.

I guess they have become friends.

Watching them walk away, right next to each other, laughing and touching, you would never know they'd just met. They looked like they *belonged* next to each other. Like they had been friends for years. They looked like they had a friendship I could truly be jealous of. Like the one I was starting to have with Jimmy and Ocean. I wondered how many people whose lives I was jealous of or even wished I had, were really what they seemed to be at all.

"Pretty girl," I said to Ocean, pushing, wanting to see what his reaction would be. To see if they were just friends or if he knew her like I did.

"She's alright."

"Who is she? Do you like her?"

He smiled. "Yeah, I like her enough."

"Enough for what?"

"Enough for what I need her for. Hey, Perry?" he asked with his voice getting louder. "What's with the twenty fuckin' questions, huh?"

"No, no," I said backtracking. "I just think she's pretty. I don't give a fuck about her though."

He started laughing.

"Bullshit. You want me to set you guys up? You could stare at her all night with those big puppy dog eyes, making kissy faces for hours and never doing anything about it."

"Yeah right."

He started laughing his fuckin' ass off.

"Why are you being like this? I just said I thought she was pretty. That's it…"

"She's a fuckin' whore, Perry. Half the guys I know have fucked her. Alright? All you gotta do is buy her a couple of drinks and feed her some sugar and she'll fuck you. That's all. That's why she's good enough tonight. Tomorrow, it'll be like I never knew her. She'll be a memory."

"Oh," I said.

He pulled on his cigarette and laughed some more.

"So maybe you should mind your own business and stop falling in love with every fuckin' girl you talk to, Perry."

"Bullshit, I don't…"

"You don't what? You telling me that you don't have a hard-on for both these whores right now? Huh?"

"No, I just…"

"Listen. If I were you I'd be less concerned about this little cunt I'm with and more worried about the psycho bitch that *you're* with."

"Why is she a psycho?"

He paused. "Perry, you don't think it's odd that this chick you met last night, whose phone number you don't even know, whose address you don't know, who you know absolutely nothing about, is all over *you* like you're a fuckin' movie star? You don't find that strange?"

I kind of did think it was weird. She *was* a knockout. She could have any guy she wanted. Why me? The girl was stunning. Not like Smoke or Snow, who were both beautiful in their own ways. Whose suffering made them more beautiful than their faces or bodies ever could. They lived lives of loneliness. Lives lived on the outside. That's what made *them* beautiful. But Ginger was gorgeous, a complete knockout. Her eyes, her lips, her hair, she was magnificent. It *was* strange that she was so into me.

"Well maybe it is a little weird. But so what?"

"So what? So *what* Perry? Do you know what happened last night? Were you there? The bitch set you up. She was all over you right when he just *happened* to walk in."

He was talking about Shadow Man. I could barely listen. He was pulling what was left of me apart, slowly. Piece by piece. Breaking me down.

"*He* was probably who she was talking to on the phone outside. The person she told to meet her there. 'And *hurry*,' she said. Remember?"

I nodded. That was what she said.

"You don't think *she wanted* him to walk in and see you two talking and kissing and shit? Hell, she was counting on it. She was also probably counting on *me* doing something to the guy after they started arguing. I mean she probably knew that you were a chicken shit from the second she saw you."

But that's not what she told me, asshole. I pulled on my smoke and looked down.

He put his hand on my shoulder. "Honestly Perry, do you think you're taking this girl home with you tonight? Do you think she's gonna let you fuck her? I mean, c'mon. She thinks you're harmless."

I caught Ocean's eyes watching something behind me and I turned, sweating. The girls had returned.

"What's up? What happened to you?" Ginger asked, rubbing the corners of my eyes.

"Nothing. It was just something he said. A joke. I was laughing."

"Oh," she replied, uninterested.

The four of us pushed up against the bar in a line, Ginger and Snow in the middle and Ocean and myself on the outsides. The girls ordered drinks and shots and pulled up close to us almost in unison. I felt sick and tiny.

Ginger glanced over at Snow and Ocean. "I think she really likes him. She couldn't stop talking about him in the bathroom."

"Really?"

"Yeah. Do you think he likes her? Did he say anything when we were gone?"

I wanted to tell Ginger that to Ocean, Snow was a fuckin' joke. A one-night stand who, because of her past, would never be taken seriously. He didn't *like her.* He liked her *enough* for what he needed her for. *That's what he said while you two were in the bathroom and she was professing her love for that asshole and you were laughing your ass off at me. She wasn't a girlfriend or a wife, just a whore. That's what he said.*

"No. He didn't say anything."

Ocean was such a fuckin' phony. He was kissing her on her ear and being nice to her, all the while planning, plotting, and scheming. I hate when other people lie. Not when I do, because when I do it's usually for a good reason, like not letting someone know that I didn't know something that *they* thought was common knowledge. I hate when other people lie though. Like the way the living speak of the dead after they are gone.

I pulled away from Ginger, the liar, and the victim. I stumbled over my own feet and for the first time realized how fucked up I was. I hollered over my shoulder, "I'm going to the bathroom!"

"Hey, Perry," Ocean started as I walked away. "That thing you got between your legs, it ain't just for pissin' you know."

I tasted my stomach.

Ocean, Snow, and Ginger burst out laughing. *Ginger* was laughing and leaning towards Ocean, like she liked him more than me. She *did* think I was harmless.

"What's the matter, Perry? Puppy dog got your tongue?"

I turned to walk away as the laughing got louder. I was their punch line. I was red and hot and wanted to burst into flames and torch the place.

"Oh, c'mon, leave him alone," Ginger squeaked out, pitying me like I was a wounded animal, unable to fend for myself.

That's it. "Fuck you." I stuck up both my middle fingers and stared right into the mouth of the Ocean. He turned purple and I turned away.

I heard the girls laughing as I walked towards the bathroom. Whether it was at him or me, I didn't know and I didn't care. It felt good to stand up for myself.

I stood over the filthy urinal with my penis in my hand. That's right Ocean, you fuck, this thing *ain't* just for pissing. Ask Smoke or the three girls from back home who I fucked before I came here. They'd tell you.

The poisoned, crippled light struggled to stay steady, flickering on and off in spurts and creating a strobe effect as I started to pee. My urine splashed down painting the porcelain urinal a light, boring yellow. The spray hit the urine of the number of Sick Fucks that had peed before me and neglected to flush. The smell of my urine was activating the smell of the Sick Fucks' urine. It was invading me and entering my body. The sick stench flowed up and into my mouth and nose and eyes and pores. I was marinating in the urine of strange men, Sick Fucks in fact. I tried holding my nose but was all too aware that I was still welcoming huge breaths of strange men's urine into my lungs through my mouth. I felt sick. Every cell in my body was being energized by strange men's urine. I was living off of it, surviving on it. *This is too much! I cannot take this…*I stopped…I had to…I held it in…in mid-piss.

The pain scared me. It actually hurt so much, it scared the shit out of me. I thought I ruptured the hose between my balls and my ass. I pictured the urine leaking out and seeping into my bloodstream. It would flow into my veins and travel through my heart, causing it to stop. I'd be the first person ever to die from a self-induced, urine-caused cardiac arrest.

That's not the way I want it to happen.

After a few cautious moments, I started to pee again. Everything worked fine and the steady flow made the pain go away. Still, I was bathing in strange men's urine. I might as well have been drinking it.

I finished. This episode was over. The light flickered on and off. I zipped up and turned away looking down at my pants to see if I had peed on myself at all and was smashed across my chest by someone that blew me off my feet and backwards into the stall behind me. My head slammed into the metal and I felt my top teeth sink into my bottom lip, disappearing and nearly touching the bottom teeth through the tissue. I fell down. My face slammed against the soiled, urine-drenched floor. I saw the blood spreading out along the cold tile beneath my face. I looked up to see who had landed me there, broken and dazed and bleeding. The figure was hazy through my foggy eyes.

Maybe Shadow Man had found me.

Birth

I struggled to breathe, writhing around in the filth and blood and urine with the wind knocked out of me. I gasped for breath like a fish on the floor of a boat. Blood was everywhere along the tile, being smeared by my hands and shirtsleeves and down my chin and onto my neck. A thick, syrupy beard, sliding down my throat, poisoning me with a part of myself. My eyes filled with tears and I realized that I was all alone with no one I knew with me.

I felt huge hands on my shoulders. My attacker had been standing over me the entire time watching me wish I was anywhere but there, bleeding. The bullshit light's fear of commitment was becoming more and more evident as it wouldn't stay either on or off for more than a few seconds at a time. The man spun me around furiously, lifted me up, and threw me against the dead wall. My teeth clenched for the impact as my body slammed. I was face to face with him with my eyes closed and blood-soaked hands in front of me to protect against another blow.

"You little fuckin' prick," a familiar voice growled. "Perry c'mon, open your eyes."

I knew the voice. I knew the hands. I knew the temper. I opened my eyes and Ocean stood before me.

"You alright?" He asked with me staring at him blankly. "C'mon, say something, you little fuck."

His voice was thunder a few inches from my face. I stared into his eyes. I wanted to curl up inside them and sleep. They were cold and barely alive, but that's where I felt I *needed* to sleep, among *the almost*, almost dead, almost alive. I could see myself swimming through his black pupils, pulling off my skin like a soiled prom dress and eating my organs from the inside out, the blood becoming delicious just as the blood in my mouth had become delicious. I was so aware of it in my veins, racing and splashing and crying beneath my hopeless skin. I could feel the blood swallow my brain. It filled my erection. It squeezed and nearly exploded out of my ears and through my eyes. I pushed my bleeding face towards his and kissed him, leaving a bloody outline around his thin lips. He jumped back. The lights went out and back on. He released his grip on my shoulders, forcing my head to slam backwards into the wall. I felt fire shoot through my skull. My body started to crumble as I turned towards the wall, attempting to hold myself up. The alcohol and the misery weighed too much and I slid down. With my left cheek scraping along the rough spackle, I saw that someone had written in black pen,

    FOR A GOOD TIME
    CALL JESUS.

I was over the sink with freezing cold water being splashed up into my face by his rough, sandpaper hands. A group of guys had surrounded us.

"What are you looking at? Wipe your hands on your shirts and beat it," he told them.

He wiped my face with coarse paper towels. I reached up to help him do it more gently. I was dizzy and my legs were made of jelly, but not a delicious kind. My stomach tasted like pea soup.

"C'mon Perry, pick your head up. Let me see you," Ocean

pleaded as my thousand-pound head swung around following my shoulders. Blood sprayed everywhere. "C'mon bro, snap out of it." His blurry words seeped into the beige walls and disappeared.

I felt myself losing. I needed to close my eyes.

I am a coma.

"C'mon P… C'mon," he said, scared as hell.

Just then I heard a girl's voice cut through the buzzing.

"What the fuck happened?! What'dya do to him?!"

It was Ginger.

"Nothing! Nothing!"

"Nothing?! He's covered in blood!"

"I know! I just came in to scare him a bit. I pushed him, softly, and he, he must've hit his head or something. He bit his lip. He just started bleeding and bugging out."

Ocean gave his side of the story. Even through the haze I didn't buy it.

"Bullshit!" I screamed.

"What? Perry, can you hear me?" Ginger was squeezing my arm.

"P., c'mon, wake up," Ocean said, holding me like a baby.

I heard people gathering. The vultures were circling.

"Here, hold him for a second." Ocean put me off into Ginger's arms.

The lights went off and back on.

I watched him, through slits, walk to the door and settle down the few guys who'd been waiting to use this bathroom. Snow was there, too. She looked sick at the sight of me. I smiled at her.

Ocean started back towards me. The light, now on for a second, off for a second, gave the impression that he wasn't walking or moving but posing differently each time I got to see him. It was like someone took twenty pictures of him and I was seeing them one by one as he drew closer. I realized as I started becoming more and more alive that *he did this* to me. Joke or not, he had hurt me. I'd been nothing but nice to this guy and all night he'd made fun of me and humiliated me and now he'd hurt me. The lights were buzzing louder to compete with the voices of the growing crowd, sneaking their heads in to see what happened. *How dare he hurt me. I never hurt anybody and I don't deserve this.* I shook with anger. He came upon me and stepped out of the dark and into the light. I looked at him and swung with my life and punched him across the left side of his face. His neck snapped to the right and his whole face contorted as everyone gasped in shock, their hands over their mouths in disbelief. I'd struck the monster. My hand throbbed. Everyone looked at me with wide eyes and still faces.

The expression on Ginger's face was different. In fact, I don't think I'll ever forget it. Her lips were bright red and she had blood—my blood—all over her and she was laughing. She nodded her head to me while her eyes flickered green to red and back to green. She was proud of me. Like Mom would be. I smiled and looked away for a moment and caught a glimpse of Ocean.

I don't know what it feels like to get struck by lightning but I'd imagine it feels a lot like this.

The fastest thing that's *ever* happened, happened right then when Ocean, who never even came close to going down from my punch, flew at me and grabbed me by the throat and threw me into the mirror on the wall. *He is a fired bullet. He is a speeding car. He is an exploding star.* My head smacked the fuckin' thing and it blew up and shattered all over me. His hand was as big as a baseball glove and he was choking me with it. With all my strength I couldn't move it even an inch. It only lasted for a second as Ginger pulled on Ocean and convinced him to back off. Then she jumped in front of me as he stood furiously staring.

"Hey! You got what you deserved!" She was pointing at him. "You started it. He just gave you back a little of what you gave him."

He didn't seem convinced. He opened and closed his fists and looked through Ginger into me. I was totally awake at this point. I was still drunk, sitting in the sink, covered in glass with blood all over my shirt and hands and who knows where else, but still I was awake. My hand was wrecked from hitting him.

He looked like he was about to lunge again when Snow stepped in and gave him a kiss on the mouth. "Stop it. C'mon, you guys are friends. Besides, he's drunk."

He took turns looking at her, and then at me, and then at her until finally he chuckled and the room breathed. He rubbed his jaw and smiled at me. "Nice punch, P... No big deal," he said, reaching his hand out to me. I shook it.

No big deal to him. But *for me* it was a big deal. I felt all the power and energy in the entire world flowing through me as I woke from the coma. The lights were back on, buzzing. I spun to see myself in the mirror. Although I was covered in blood that had seeped from my swollen bottom lip, I looked more alive than I had in months. My eyes were blue like the water in a place I'd never been and never will. My cheeks were red. They looked healthy. . .I was fine. I was beautiful. Ocean stared at the beautiful me. He spoke.

"You alright man?"

"Yeah. Are you?"

He laughed. He gave me a blast. Then another.

I smacked into a wall of music and broke it down. I destroyed every fuckin' note that bled from the speakers. I inhaled perfume and blew out gasoline and lit all the alcohol on fire. A trillion years of smoke became a tornado that screamed up into the ceiling. The dead surrounded me and played ring-around-the-rosy as I fell in and out of other dimensions. I walked in slow motion. Everyone turned.

I am a super hero. I am a rock star.

The four of us walked up to the bar. I stared off into the mirror behind it. I was covered in blood. I was smiling my ass off.

Ginger rubbed my back. I sipped on my beer as everything returned to normal for them. But for me, for me, I got a taste of it. That fight with Ocean changed something inside of me. I felt alert, prepared, ready to act. I wasn't just the author of the story, I was a character like all the rest. I'd gone from dead to alive in the smelly, shitty bathroom and I was ready for anything.

Up on the TV over the bar I watched footage of an escaped elephant trampling people in the street outside of a zoo or circus or wherever. I love when that shit happens, when an elephant freaks out after years of humiliation and goes on a rampage. That elephant whose been broken and trained to stand on his back legs or wear ridiculous costumes so Big Shots and Sick Fucks can laugh, eat popcorn, and pretend their heads aren't filled with violent sexual perversions, that elephant broke through fences and ran down the slow and the weak. He ignored the trainers that for years had been egotistical enough to think that they could actually control an elephant. Out on the street the elephant screamed, with no words, *I am not here for your fuckin' amusement!! I need respect and I refuse to be humiliated any more.* The elephant was just like me when I stood up to Ocean. Our days as a joke and a punchline bubbled over and erupted in both of us finally standing up for ourselves. I told Ocean to fuck off, and the elephant burst onto the street and barreled head-on into cars and walls and whatever. He was just like me. We were the same.

"Hey let's go. We're leaving," Ginger said, bringing my attention back to the bar and to all the people staring at me in my dried blood mask.

"Yeah, okay." I looked up at the screen a final time as I started to follow her out. I wanted to get one last glimpse of the elephant that was just like me. He was on the ground. He was just like me. The police stood over him with guns and erections. He was just like me. They killed him. We were the same.

It was freezing outside, and we were all under-dressed. It was three A.M., and I didn't want the night to end. I kept thinking about what Ocean had said about me not being able to go home with Ginger, about how she was using me and would never fuck me. I hoped he was wrong.

"So what do you want to do now?" I asked Ginger.

She paused. "Uh, well, there is an after-hours place downtown. It'll just be getting started by the time we get there. If you guys want to go."

"Hey P., you sure you can hang? You don't have to get back to your brother's?" Ocean asked nicely. Not sarcastic at all.

Alex wasn't even there and Andrea could probably care less. She's nice and all, but fuck her. She's not what I was thinking about. I wanted Ginger to *really* ask me like she wanted me to come.

"You can stay by me if you want," Ocean said, even nicer than the first time. He was so fuckin' two-faced.

"Well, what about that?" Snow asked, grabbing and stretching out my shirt, showing the blood and looking at Ginger.

There was silence as we all watched our breath turn white and float away in the cold. Snow dropped the shirt and disappeared, tucked under Ocean's arm, holding him tightly around his waist, trying to stay warm. She had no idea that he could care less. Ginger lit up a cigarette. So did Ocean. So did I. Ginger walked over and lifted off my shirt. She flipped it inside out and put it back on as I froze. She took a handkerchief out of her bag and wet it with her mouth. She began cleaning the blood off of my chin and neck.

"C'mon Perry," she said. "He said you can stay by him, so what's the big deal?"

MERCURY MAN

The gray and black smoked-out apartment sat above a tattoo parlor. The Hipsters all stared at us through their bullshit glasses and their massive loneliness, but I guess figured we had to know *someone* to be there, so they looked away and continued speaking about nothing and death. I slammed two beers on the subway and felt myself getting drunk for the second time that night. Twice in one night is nothing. Sometimes I can get drunk three or four times in one night.

The party looked like a scene out of a movie I've never seen or heard of. There were about twenty people, mostly guys, leaning against things, and talking incessantly. It was late, 3:30 by then, but I didn't care about time.

I don't sleep. I don't eat. I don't believe.

Ocean was in the fridge throwing us cans of beer that didn't belong to us—one each for me, Snow, Ginger, and himself. I took a sip. It was stale and barely cold. I forced myself to pound it. I held my nose so I couldn't taste. My stomach was bloated and felt as if it was going to burst, but still I downed the whole thing and stole another.

Ginger slowly drifted away from our group. The others kept talking as I watched her. She walked up to a guy with very pale skin and very short yellow hair. He looked a bit like a fluorescent lightbulb with a shirt on. I named him Glow. She whispered something in his ear and they turned and walked to a door on the wall. They opened it and slid inside.

No one noticed what I noticed. I was the only one not caught up in everything that was happening. Pot smoke flooded my nose and mouth and I started coughing. Snow and Ocean stood in line to receive a joint from the dirtiest girl I'd ever seen in my whole life. It'd been a few minutes and Ginger still wasn't back. My stomach burned like hell and my palms were sweating.

In the midst of everything, someone flipped a light switch and the whole room went black except for a few posters on the walls and everyone's teeth and eyes.

"Hey Perry," Snow said with a ghost's mouth, "do you want some?" She held the joint up to me. It burned ivory-white beneath the black light. I took it and pulled hard and nearly coughed to death.

"Where'd she go?" I asked Snow after I caught my breath.

She shrugged.

I took another hard pull off the joint. I finished my beer and grabbed another one. Ocean poured some coke on his hand in the middle of the kitchen. He blew it up. He poured some on my hand and I did the same. The joint made its way back to me and I hit it hard. I coughed my ass off.

Ten minutes went by. Ginger was still missing. The voices spun around me and out of control. The sick white mouths of all these fucks were wide open, letting poison back into the already polluted world. I could see every piece of lint and fuzz on all of their clothes and my own. I was picking at it as they kept laughing. Picking. Laughing. Picking. I got disoriented: The lights, the laughing, the whole scene itself. Someone bumped me and spilled some beer on me.

I spun to my right and grabbed an empty beer bottle off the windowsill. I flew toward the door that Ginger had disappeared inside of. I banged on it, hard. Half the party turned and looked at me.

"One second," Glow said.

I banged again. Glow flung open the door. His pants were unbuttoned.

"What the fuck, man?!"

I looked past him and saw Ginger sitting on the toilet seat. There were half-snorted lines on the back of a CD case.

"You got a fuckin' problem man?!"

I didn't answer. Well, not with words. I spit in his face and slammed the thick end of the bottle across the side of his head. The bottle exploded and he fell back onto the blue bathmat. Ginger jumped up and spread herself flat against the back wall. I jumped on top of him and slammed my fist into his face so hard and so fast that his nose broke and expanded out wide like spread jelly. The blue mat was becoming red beneath his bashed head and face. Someone grabbed me from behind and spun me around and out the door. I followed my momentum and flew through the shocked party, down the steps, skipping half of them, out the door and onto the street.

I breathed from my chest with my face burning off from the sting of the cold. I couldn't feel my right hand. I didn't know where I was or where to go. I walked left down the street. It looked familiar, so I pushed on despite being a freezing cold wreck.

My right hand is a locomotive.

I got to the corner and the sign read Sullivan Street. It might as well have read *Bullshit Outer Space Street* because I had no idea which way I needed to go anyway.

I put up my bloody hand to hail a cab. Streams of tears fell out of me from exhaustion, sorrow, and just being someone who believes so strongly in not believing in himself that misery consumes his life. *I am addicted to it. I live for it. I am going to die for it. I will not be stopped.*

I heard someone call my name.

"Perry!"

It was a girl. I ignored the voice and faced forward, praying for a cab to take me away. I was crying and didn't want anyone to see me like that.

"Perry!!"

The voice was louder this time and accompanied by footsteps running towards me. It was Ginger, I could tell.

"Hey," she said, spinning me around. She looked at me...at my tears.

"I have to go," I said.

"What, back to your brother's? I'll go with you."

"No, not back to my brother's. I don't belong there. I don't belong here."

"Oh c'mon Perry, stop being so hard on yourself. You're just tired, that's all. Here," she said, putting her pinky nail inside a small bag of sugar, scooping some out, and putting it up to my nose.

We were standing in the middle of the street.

"That was incredible, what you did back there."

"Who was that fuckin' guy?"

"He was an asshole whose face you fuckin' smashed in! That was sick, Perry."

"Yeah?"

"Yeah."

She seemed so happy that the guy was suffering. She started walking towards me and I stepped back a few steps. She put her hand up to me. She still had the coke on her fingernail. I inhaled it.

"C'mon. Let's go," she said.

Her apartment was small and very messy. I don't know why but I thought it would be different—maybe bigger, cleaner. It was six in the morning, but I was wide awake looking at all the paintings on the wall.

"I painted those," she said, noticing me staring.

"Really, really? They're really nice. I didn't know…"

"It's just a hobby," she interrupted. "It's nothing serious."

She seemed like she didn't want to talk about it, even after she brought it up. She seemed so proud at first, then embarrassed. She was bright red and not looking at me. I'd never seen her embarrassed like that. It made her seem a bit more human. Like, she wasn't just some cartoon character, numbed and running.

I plopped down on the bed. "Hey, what's that one?"

It was a painting that covered almost the entire wall next to her bed. It was the sun with a man's face painted lightly over it. There were planets spread out behind and around it, all with faces painted lightly on them. I asked her about it. She was uncomfortable. I kind of liked that.

"Oh. That's nothing. Just something I did recently."

"Yeah, but it's real cool."

"Really? You really like it?"

She pulled up the shades and looked out at the early morning sky. She watched for a few moments. The sun was buried, as it had been for days. She turned to me and, with wet eyes and lips, got up onto the bed right in my face. She leaned in and kissed me. I kissed back. She tasted like candy and poison. I put my hands on her waist. She pushed them away. The polluted daylight poked its head in and she pulled back.

She reached over and took a small mirror out of her desk drawer and placed it on the bed. She chopped up two thick lines. "Slug trails," she called them; they were so thick that they resembled the trail a slug leaves on your front porch in the summer. She handed me a drinking straw that she'd cut in half. She held the mirror up to my face. I inhaled the sugar and shivered. She did the same.

"Perry, do you really want to know about this painting?" she asked, closing her eyes and running her fingers along it. Her nails scraping made me clench my teeth. "Huh? Do you want to know?"

"Yes."

"Okay, go over there."

I moved over by the painting as she directed with her fingers.

"Now, turn and face the window with your head where the sun is on the wall."

I turned with my back to the painting and my face towards the window. Slices of gray morning sneaked in with every moment that passed.

"Close your eyes and spread your arms like this."

She lifted my shirt up over my head and pushed my arms down from my biceps until they were spread out at my sides. I got freaked and began trying to hold in my stomach. I had a hard-on. I felt her moving around on the bed. She straddled me and kissed my lips and I opened my eyes. My bottom lip stung. My heart raced and my skull buzzed. She put her fingers over my lids and closed them again. The new day brought more rain. It slammed against the fire escape. Still the world was getting brighter as the last few drops of black night dissolved into the eternally gray sky.

I dwell in the world of soft kisses and sugar cane.

"So what about the painting?"

"Okay. Let's see," she said, shoving me back into position against the wall. I sat Indian style.

"Hmm. *Who* are you Perry Patton?"

"What?"

"Sshh. *Who* are you? Are you Jupiter, king of the gods?" she asked, lifting my left hand up at a forty-five-degree angle. "Nope. But I think I already knew that."

My hand dropped.

"Are you a warrior?" She lifted my right arm up completely over my head. "Well, it's clear that you can be, but no, you're a sweetheart. So you're not Mars." This time, she whispered right into my ear.

My hand dropped.

"Now you're not Venus."

"Why not?"

"Because Venus is a woman, silly."

"Oh."

"Hmmm. Are you evil Perry? Are you the god of the Underworld?" She stretched my left hand all the way up and to my left. I dropped it right away.

"I didn't think so."

She paused. The rain beat down.

"You know, you just came to town and already my life is different. Twice you got me out of situations that I shouldn't have been in. Maybe you were *sent* here. Maybe you were *sent* here and you don't even know it. So you could be a messenger."

Her lips were right up on mine.

"Messenger from who?"

"Sshh."

She lifted both of my hands directly over my head until they touched in the middle.

"Perry, I have a feeling you are going to be here and gone very quickly. I think I'm right. Right?"

"Yes."

"Yeah, you'll be moving on very quickly."

She made a few final adjustments as I sat Indian style with my arms stretched out directly above me and my hands touching.

She pulled back and I opened my eyes.

"So what now?"

She walked over to the window. Again she stared out and up. She leaned her entire body out the window and kicked her feet as they became airborne. She turned back to me and smiled. Then she pulled a cord with her right hand and a huge black cloth dropped down in front of the window. The room went nearly all black except for a million scattered beams of dull light that sneaked through a million pinholes in the cloth. They flickered on me and on the painting and a ton of other random points on the walls. The light shook because the cloth hadn't yet settled. Also some of the holes must've had colored paper or filters in them because red, green, and blue beams trembled and shimmered everywhere.

Ginger hopped up on the bed and put something cold in my hands. "Hold it just like this. Don't move."

She walked over to the radio and turned the volume up, loud. Elvis Costello barreled through. "Are you ready, Perry?"

"Yes."

She walked along the walls in the darkness, opening the bathroom door, then the closet. They had mirrors inside. The lights shot off the mirrors and hit the object she had put in my hands. It was a prism. It was reflecting light back at different mirrors. The lights then bounced off those mirrors. The entire room was covered in frozen ropes of light and color that cut and crossed and ran alongside and atop each other. It was the most amazing thing I had ever seen in my whole life.

Ginger hopped back up onto my lap. I dropped the prism and all the lights fell.

"Oh no, you can't drop your hands. They're in the perfect place. Right in front of Mercury."

I looked up as she replaced them softly. She put them right in front of planet Mercury on the painting. She then put the prism in my hands and the lights jumped back and forth through the air. It was even more beautiful than the first time. She pulled up close to me and licked my bottom lip. She licked it where it had been bleeding. I started to drop my hands and she jumped up and fixed them. Then she stretched my legs out straight. She started kissing my chest, neck, and shoulders, all the while keeping my hands steady in the spot that made the colors fly. With the music blaring and the room spinning, she pulled open my zipper. She made sure I kept my hands above my head. She pulled her underwear off from underneath her skirt and sat on top of me. She was soaked; I slid right in. She leaned in as she began grinding against me.

"Ask me anything," she said with her eyes closed.

"About what?"

"Anything."

I wanted to ask a million things. I wanted to ask about the guy at the party. Or about Shadow Man. Instead I whispered, "Why me?"

"*Why you* what?"

"Why me, right now? Before? Yesterday? Out of every guy in this whole city, why me?"

She started smiling with her eyes closed.

I was having trouble holding my hands up, but every time I tried to drop them, she stopped me. She was so beautiful. I couldn't believe I was inside of her. It was something that nobody could take away from me, ever.

"You really want to know?" she said, leaning down and grinding even harder.

"Yes," I squeaked out.

She started bucking even harder. I knew I couldn't hold out much longer. I was going to get off at any moment and my arms were exhausted from being held above my head. She was breathing so heavy, right on top of me. I could feel my pubic hair drenched and matted. She started coming.

"Come with me, inside of me," she said. Rocking up and down and wheezing in and out, she exploded inside a world of lights and mirrors and I exploded inside of her.

I put my hands down as she fell onto my chest. The light show ceased. She lay on me, with her hands on my sides, breathing deeply, looking away. I was still inside her.

We breathed without talking for a few minutes, until she spoke into my chest. "Do you still want to know *why you?*"

"Yes."

She looked up at me. I found it funny how small and afraid she looked then, as though too much of her had been revealed and now she had to hide from sight.

"It's because you are The Mercury Man. You are the messenger."

Robots

It was getting harder to separate the days. I wasn't sleeping. I was barely eating. I was drinking and smoking and snorting myself to death. I had no schedule, no direction. I could have easily crawled into any small space, closed my eyes, slept for days, and awakened just as dazed and demented. I wasn't able to remember what it was like to feel healthy and fun and awake. I'd walked around the city in the few days I'd been there in a perpetual haze of dull headaches and drunken dreams. I felt no different after eight hours of sleep than I did when I'd stayed up all night. I had no concept of time or day or date. Whatever it said on the wall, I'd believe.

8:45 A.M. That sounded right.

I know that everyone knows I've been up all night. I know that everyone on the streets and in the deli know what I did last night. It's by the way they're watching. *I am a criminal. I am a deviant.*

"What'll it be, buddy?"

"Sesame bagel with butter," I replied to the middle-aged clerk with the accusing eyes and the chewed pencil behind his ear. Probably a number-two pencil; that seems to be *the pencil.* I wonder what happened to number-one pencils. I'll bet the people that made them never saw that coming. They were probably banking on number-one pencils being *the pencil.* Somewhere along the line, though, people decided on the number twos. It's kind of like all the people who years ago thought that *Tito* Jackson was the horse to bet on. I guess you never know. Anyway, if he didn't watch it, I was gonna poke his fuckin' asshole eyes out with that pencil. I swear.

I stood at the counter. Crazed Big Shots and Dolls raced by and around me. All these Big Shots were scrambling to be at their desks by nine. I wouldn't move for them. I hated them. *Robots.* I turned to get a drink from the freezer and saw a long and thin reflection of myself in the metal that surrounded the glass. My lip was fatty and plump and purple and still had dried blood trailing away from it and onto my neck. My hair was a mess. My shirt, which I had put back on right side out when I left Ginger's, was wrinkled and covered in blood. *I'm so pretty.*

I stood out front eating my bullshit bagel and sipping on a small carton of O.J. It was still raining but the sun was struggling to peek through the clouds.

Ginger had to go to work. She showered and went on no sleep. She kissed me when she left. I followed her directions perfectly and was right across the street from Alex and Andrea's apartment. I didn't want to go in. He'd still be out of town but even so, I didn't like being there. I didn't feel welcome. It was hard because in my heart I loved Alex and I think he loved me back but I just think if you act a certain way long enough it gets too hard to change. It's like sometimes it feels like it easier to say *I love you* to someone you barely know than it is to say it to someone you've known forever. Life is fucked up like that.

The sun came out from behind a cloud and I stared right into it. My eyes watered and I had to look away. I got nauseous and dizzy and did it again. And again. And again until my eyes were burning, the world looked gray, and I felt sick. I was beginning to like things better in gray anyway. The sun went away. I wouldn't see it again.

Some guy in a blue BMW was wiping bird shit off of his

windshield. He looked at me. "Fuckin' disgusting, huh? They should all be shot," he said.

It's so funny, all us fucks running around all day, in fancy clothes and fancy cars, popping fancy pills and eating fancy meals, while birds fly and sing and laugh their asses off, shitting on all of us, shitting on awnings and porches and toupees and, of course, our cars. We drive around with bird shit marking our car windows and hoods. But I think we get off lucky. I'd love to see what the birds could do if they combined their efforts and all over the world, all shit at once. They could drown us in oceans of it. They should. We deserve it. We would be up to our necks, barely able to breathe or keep our heads above it. Some of us would be washed away as rivers of bird shit flowed down every street in every city, drenching and engulfing the prestigious and the elite. People just like these Big Shot vermin here, running to get to jobs that make no difference to anyone, anywhere. Running to hide in places where small men with small voices speak small words in small doses to gossiping women with pointy noses, fake nails, and halitosis, who tell their kids lies, laughing when the bedroom door closes, about Superman, Santa Claus, and God. People running around thinking that the birds are disgusting because of the way nature has made them, while the really disgusting things happen not in the sky with the birds, but in the bathrooms of all these folks.

They're all covering up the disgusting things they do with colognes and deodorants and feminine sprays. But I know better: All these people, meeting and conversing on the streets and in offices, trying desparately to pretend that they didn't just come from doing very disgusting things in very disgusting ways in very disgusting places. Women with bleeding, stinking cunts. Men belching and farting and shitting horrendous brown sewage that splashes up and soaks their big fat asses. At least the birds make no bones about it. They fly, they eat, they shit, sometimes all at the same time. While we, the *civilized*, run from shitting and bleeding and picking our noses and rubbing our balls and then smelling our fingers so we can smell our balls, to bars to meet people of the opposite sex, pretending we are interested in good company and good conversation but really much more interested in indulging in violent sex acts involving jellies and creams and leather. Pretending we are not disgusting is like pretending we do not breathe or eat. At least the birds admit it. It doesn't matter to me though. I don't fucking like birds anyway. They're just flying rodents.

I barely noticed how messed up my bed was before I collapsed and melted into the mattress. I kicked my shoes off while I laid there. I put my left hand under my head, beneath the pillow, to feel the cold side. I scrunched my entire body together and then stretched out long like a cat, my muscles elastic and shaking, releasing the tension. I was exhausted and bruised and covered in Ginger. I didn't wash myself off at her apartment because *I wanted* her all over me.

Alex's place was empty.

My eyes were closed, but I couldn't sleep. The events of last night raced through my head: the fight with Ocean, the party above the tattoo shop, Ginger disappearing with Glow, me punishing him for it, and finally her having sex with me in the midst of a meteor shower. She was a goddess kissing and then laying down with a man. *I am undeserving.* And when she called me The Mercury Man, the messenger, I didn't know what to think. It's why she said she slept with me. It's *why* everything.

I would start to doze off and then pop back to life when

something inside me would scare something else inside me enough to put off resting a bit longer. I thought about how helpless I was when I slept. How anyone could do anything to me. How people could be plotting and scheming in my house or Alex's apartment while I lay soft, unconscious, and unaware. *I am so helpless.* We all are. So vulnerable, so often, lying to the world about our strength and courage. Spending hours every night laying still with bull's-eyes painted on our skulls, taunting and enticing sledgehammer-wielding psychopaths wearing dark trench coats.

The man with the dark coat and heavy hammer lifts it above his head. His silhouette is massive against the back wall with the family photos on it as the light from the street lamp that is desperately wanting to scream and call for help shines in. He is never seen, never heard, never caught as his stomach clenches and he brings down, with every last bit of strength he has, a screaming sledgehammer into...

The phone rang and I jumped up, sweating and gasping for breath and covering my head with my hands. I tried to figure out where I was and whether I was still alive or just pretending to be. It rang again and I jumped up, this time wishing more than anything that I was fuckin' deaf and unable to hear anything. I picked it up. It was Mom.

"Perry, how are you?"

I was shaking.

"I'm fine. What time is it?"

"Nine fifteen."

I was silent.

"At night," she said. "Were you napping?"

"Yeah, yeah I was," I replied, trying to figure how I slept for the past twelve hours without anyone doing anything horrible to me.

I was having trouble breathing. I started to hyperventilate.

"Perry, I know you are grown up now and you are trying to do things on your own, but I want you to know that I love you very much and really wish I could be there with you."

I didn't speak.

"I really do Perry…"

"Really?"

I was really having trouble breathing. I started rummaging through my bag looking for a drink, something to calm me.

"Yes, Perry. You should come home. I'm worried about you."

"I'm worried too, Mom."

"So get on the next train home. You'll be home and safe before you know it."

"I can't. I'm sorry, Mom, I can't."

"Perry, I love you and be care—"

I hung up before she finished. I looked up at her picture on my wall and again it was different. All the colors were gone. All the colors that I'd pressed into paper all those years ago had escaped; greens, reds, browns, blues, blacks, and yellows on the loose, scampering to find dullness to brighten up. They were off to attach to sweaters and streetlights and storefronts and lipsticks and fire hydrants and tattoos and to drown in the sky. But they were mine, my colors, and it killed me that they were gone.

I pulled three miniature bottles of whiskey out of my bag. I swallowed half the first bottle and laid down. My chest was expanding and contracting as I tried to breathe bigger. I had chains around my torso getting tighter each time I exhaled. I started to feel as if the bed was spinning out of control and I had to hold on tight to keep from being thrown off. It's like I stopped believing in gravity at the same time it stopped believing in me and I was fighting from falling upwards into the black sky. *I am an astronaut lost in space.*

I laid on the bed with my eyes closed, taking sips of whiskey every ten seconds. Counting, one, two, three…and at ten I'd drink with my nose closed so I couldn't taste. I did this until they were all empty and I was numb.

I poked my head out the door to see if anyone was around. The apartment was desolate. I strolled out and opened the fridge. It didn't matter. I wasn't hungry. Plus the bullshit food looked like it could've been poisoned. I lit up a cigarette. The smoke barreled down my throat and into my lungs. I felt calm.

Out of the corner of my eye I noticed that the dining room table that was usually quite cluttered with Alex's bullshit legal papers was completely clean except for one piece of loose leaf paper. I checked it out.

Perry,
Went to the movies. Alex will be home tonight. Would love to talk about a few things. How about tomorrow around dinnertime?
Andrea

I was supposed to meet Ginger at 11:00. It was only 10:15 so I stumbled into a little dive bar on the way to the other bar. It seems like there are always bars on the way to other bars. In this city at least.

I ordered a whiskey. The woman next to me was skinny and smiling with big lips painted over much smaller lips. She was older, probably forty, and she looked sick. Her skin didn't fit right, it was loose, too loose, and her eyes were bright red and watery, floating in the sockets. She was smoking.

My hands trembled from the cold. I took a sip, then another. I got the chills and burped. Another sip and another. Half of my drink was gone. Another swig. This one felt like it was going to come back up. I steadied myself. For the next one, I held my nose closed so I wouldn't taste it. One huge swig and I finished it and slammed the glass down on the bar.

"Can I have another one?" I said to the bartender.

He turned to get it.

"How about one for me, too?" the sick woman next to me asked, slurring her words.

"Yeah right," I mumbled under my breath.

"Oh c'mon, a young, handsome guy like you, you can buy a drink for a pretty lady like myself."

"Leave him alone, Tina," the bartender said.

The woman, who I named *Skin Bag*, for obvious reasons, seemed all right. At the very least, she was trying to destroy herself like me. "Get her whatever she wants," I said.

I do Big Shot stuff sometimes.

"Thanks, cutie. Richie, double Jack straight."

The bartender looked at me like I was crazy or at the very least pouring gasoline on a fire that he had been trying to put out for a while.

"You want one?" she asked, holding her pack of smokes out towards me while one unlit cigarette dangled between her lips.

Skin Bag handed me a cigarette and I put it between my dry, slightly chapped lips. She put her lighter up to my face. She ran her thumb over the wheel and it ignited, warming my left eye, eyelid, and lashes. I went to light the cigarette and the fire went out. Again she ignited it and again as I went to light it, it went out.

"Sorry," I squeaked as she killed me with her eyes.

"Don't breathe out," she said as she ignited it one last time.

People that don't *breathe out* are dead, I thought, as the white tip became black and burned away.

It was a little after eleven and the cold from the gusting wind and rain flowed through every bone in my back and along my spine, despite the fact that I was bundled up tightly. Skin Bag gave me a few cigarettes for the road (I had my own but fuck it, free smokes) one of which was in my mouth, burning and shrinking with every drag I took. I sneaked into the next bar.

Ginger was nowhere to be found, so I ordered a beer and lit up another cigarette. I was pretty buzzed when Jimmy tapped me on the shoulder. He smelled great.

"Whoa, hey man. What's going on?"

I was shocked to see him there. It felt like it had been forever since we'd hung out but I guess it had really only been a couple of days. "Let me buy you a drink," I said. "A glass of Merlot," I told the bartender, pushing my money forward.

"Thanks." He waited. "So…you getting wrecked by yourself, brother?"

"I am actually meeting someone here. A girl. The one we saw the other day outside the coffee shop."

"Really. Wow. Looks like you've got everything under control."

"Yep."

"Well, you mind if I hang out for a little while, until she shows up?"

"Not at all."

I wanted him to stay.

THE NEVER ENDERS

Eleven o'clock turned into twelve and twelve turned into one. I was drunk and Jimmy and I were smoking a pack of cigarettes I'd bought from an antique vending machine in the corner of the bar. Ginger never showed up. I called her apartment and cell numbers a few times and got no answer on either. Jimmy felt bad. *Fuck her.*

I was running my fingers through a small puddle of water and beer that had formed on the bar in front of me, tracing shapes, drawing everyone in the whole place. I created them and watched them die almost instantly as the liquid returned to its original shape the second my finger passed through.

I felt a hand on my shoulder. I put a napkin over the dead and spun around. It was Ocean. I was disappointed.

"What are you guys doing?"

"Uh…"

"Vodka tonic," he said to the bartender. "P., you want something?"

"Whiskey, please," I said to both of them.

"Jimmy?"

"Red."

"You see her anywhere? She was supposed to meet me here."

"Who?" I asked.

"*Who?* The eccentric poet, that's who. Did you forget about your first love since you've moved onto bigger and better things?"

He was talking about Smoke.

"No, I didn't. I haven't, uh, seen her that is."

"I saw her at ten downtown. She was talking to some bartender, flirting," Jimmy said.

"As usual," Ocean said.

"*As* usual. She was trying to get him to get off early…"

Ocean interrupted Jimmy. "I heard you get off early all the time. It's a big problem."

Jimmy laughed. "If she's not here, then she's with some poor guy, probably breaking his heart in half." He nudged me when he said it and smiled.

Jimmy and Ocean were laughing and joking. Whatever their bullshit problem was the night before, it was settled.

"So what, are you guys getting wrecked? Ya having a little party?" He scoped the place out, looking around and drinking his vodka.

"Yeah, I guess." I was too embarrassed to say that Ginger stood me up, so I lied.

Dirtmouth walked in. "Hey girls, the pussy man is here. Every girl line up and don't forget to bring your sweet pussies."

Man, I fuckin' like that guy.

"C'mon, let's go. There's a party uptown," Jimmy said, looking mostly at me.

I wanted to stay to see if Ginger would show. But staying would mean I would have to tell everyone, including Ocean, that she had stood me up and that was exactly what he thought would happen from the beginning so I wasn't about to do that.

We pushed through the doors of the penthouse apartment. Smoke called Jimmy's cell while we were on our way and she met us out front. We walked in, in a line. King, then Ocean, then Smoke, then Dirtmouth, then The Mercury Man. The Big Shot owner came up and hugged Jimmy hard. Jimmy sold coke to the guy. That's how he knew about the party.

His place was insane—three fuckin' floors. An *apartment* that was three fuckin' floors! The television looked like a movie screen and there was a goddamn fish tank in the wall; built into the fuckin' wall and it was big enough for Ocean to swim laps in. Paintings that were as big as bay windows covered the other walls and there was a fully stocked bar that ran down the left side of a dropped living room. There were mostly girls and a handful of guys, probably twenty-five people total, drinking and snorting coke off an enormous glass coffee table in the living room. I saw Jimmy hand the Big Shot owner a huge bag of blow in return for an even bigger wad of money.

"C'mon my people, let's party!" he screamed as he began throwing the coke all over the table in piles. Everyone scampered to hit a different pile. The hottest chicks I'd ever seen in my life were cutting up lines. Five lines here, eight lines there…it was madness. I peered into another room and saw a jacuzzi inside and there were three girls wearing bikinis with their huge fake tits hanging out. They were drinking champagne and laughing their asses off.

"Jimmy, can I get you and your friends some drinks?" the owner shouted from across the room at the bar.

I put my lips on my tenth or so drink of the night. I was exhausted and sat down on the couch next to some Spanish girl that was so hot I couldn't even deal with it.

"Do you party?" She asked me, handing me a rolled fifty-dollar bill.

"Yeah, sure."

I inhaled a huge line and looked up to see Dirtmouth and Ocean doing the same.

My exhaustion was replaced by an electric buzzing that I felt all the way down to my toes. I snorted another line. So did the Spanish girl. She put some coke on my bottom lip with her nail and leaned in and sucked it off. My lip went numb. My heart raced. My vision got fuckin' blurry as hell. The Spanish girl leaned in again and stuck her tongue in my mouth. I kissed back.

"What's your name?" I asked.

"None of your business," she said, and continued kissing me in front of everyone. "You ever do Ecstasy?"

"No."

"Here." She opened my mouth and dropped a little white pill inside. I didn't fight her.

I guzzled my whiskey and washed it down. "You're supposed to wash it down with lots of water," she said.

"I'm supposed to do a lot of things I don't do."

She smiled and asked, "Can I snort coke off your dick?"

"Right here."

"No silly, follow me."

We walked to the bathroom on the second floor. I was grinding the hell out of my teeth and blinking like a fuckin' maniac.

Inside she said, "Drop your pants."

"No, I'm not hard."

She started kissing me on my neck and rubbing my dick with the palm of her left hand. I felt it swell inside my jeans. She knelt down. She unzipped my pants. My dick burst out of my underwear, right into her face. She poured a sloppy line down the center of the top of my shaft. She made it as neat as possible with her nail. She snorted it straight through her nostril. She licked the residue off me. She ran her tongue down the length of me. I throbbed. I hoped she'd put me in her mouth. She did. I leaned back against the door. I grinded my jaw back and forth.

She swallowed me.

The hours flew by and soon it was daytime. We were still drinking and snorting and blasting fuckin' Metallica. I'd thrown up twice already. The second time it was mostly blood. I'd drink until I felt so drunk and tired that I was going to pass out and then I'd blow the sickest fuckin' line and wake my ass up. Again I'd do it and again. It was ten in the morning…eleven…one in the afternoon. We were all still awake. King, Ocean, Smoke, Dirtmouth, and The Mercury Man.

"Party never ends. Huh P.? It never fuckin' ends," Ocean slurred.

We are The Never Enders. That's who we are.

Everything was black. I dreamed I was in outer space, being sucked into a black hole. My body stretched long and thin. All my bones broke and dissolved out through my skin. My mom was there.

I opened my eyes, sweating to death from fake inside heat, stuck to the same black leather couch I'd spent most of the last day on. It was night: 9:15. Most everybody was gone. A few bodies lay scattered about the couch and floor. All the Never Enders were gone. The Spanish girl was lying on my chest. My nose was clogged. I had a ton of fuckin' phlegm in my throat. My head throbbed. I felt the blood pumping through it. The blood, trillions of razor blades cutting open the insides of my veins and arteries. I lifted the Spanish girl's arm off of me. I walked to the Big Shots' bar. I stole a bottle of whiskey.

I vomited on the street. My entire body heaved. My ribs crunched tight. I wished I broke them all.

A face, attached to a body, melted off a wall beneath a neon sign and spoke. "Be careful, son. Don't fight it."

"I'm not your fuckin' son," I said to the guy. He was homeless. He had a cart with all his shit in it.

"Be careful. I once had all the opportunity in the world and everybody loved me. And now…"

"You're a fuckin' deadbeat stalker. Get away from me."

Okay, so I truly have become an asshole.

I stopped at a payphone. The wind blew a wall of rain into my side as I ducked behind the metal partition. I pushed a handful of quarters into the slot and dialed.

"Hello."

"Hi, Mom."

"Perry, how are you?"

"Uh…I'm not great…I feel like I'm losing it."

"Perry, you need to come home. You don't sound well. It's not safe for you."

"I don't think I can. There is something I need to do."

"Perry, whatever it is, forget it. You need to come home. You need to be in a safe place, where you can be taken care of."

"I know but…"

"Perry, I miss you."

"I miss you, too."

My stomach burned when the whiskey hit it, like iodine on a skinned knee multiplied by one thousand. I pulled hard on a cigarette. I needed some coke to stay awake. I took a cab to Cherry Bar. It was pretty dead. I looked for Jimmy. I found Ocean.

"Yo, P. How the fuck are you, man? You have fun with that little senorita last night?"

"You have any coke man?" I needed to wake up or I was going to collapse on the floor.

"Of course."

I followed him into the bathroom. He stuck his apartment key in the bag and held it up to my nose. The coke balanced perfectly on the end. I hit it. I hit it again. He did one. I hit it again. Then he took another. My nose was running. I tasted the drip in the back of my throat. I dry heaved violently. He lit up a smoke and washed his hands. I had to take a crap. I hovered over the bowl and in two seconds, brown and red shit fell out of me. It had blood in it. I barely wiped my ass. I asked him for another blast.

I am a forest fire. I am a nuclear accident. I am an unnatural disaster.

It was two A.M. and I could barely see I was so tired and so fucked. "I'm leaving," I said to Ocean.

"Shit, really? I was gonna swing by this party where that chick from two nights ago is hangin' out."

He was talking about Snow.

"Really? I thought she was just a one-night stand? You know, *good enough for tonight* and all that shit."

"Hah. Yeah that's what I thought, too. But hey, if you wanna split, that's cool."

I thought about it for a second. I thought that there may be a slim chance that Ginger was there. She and Snow got pretty close the other night. They may have exchanged numbers or something. But even if she was, she stood me up. I didn't want to see her.

"Yeah, I'm outta here, man."

"Cool. Take my number. Call me tomorrow. We'll party."

Broken

I was excited the whole cab ride home that Ocean had given me his phone number. It made me feel good when people liked me. I wasn't used to it but I liked it. I forgot all about Ginger. *Fuck her. She doesn't care about me at all. I am the coldest, deadest being in the universe.*

I stepped out of the cab and sitting on the stoop of Alex and Andrea's building, shivering, was Ginger. I stopped.

"Hi," she said.

"Hi."

"Are you mad at me?"

"No, not really." I *was* mad.

"Perry, I am so sorry," she said as she jumped up. "I fell asleep after work yesterday and when I woke up it was like one in the morning. already." She was speaking very quickly. "I rushed to the bar but you were gone so I rushed over here but you never came home. I came back tonight…I've been here for hours…I'm really sorry…"

She started crying.

"Don't cry, it's not a big deal." Not now it wasn't.

"No, I'm not crying because of that, it's something else."

"What?"

"No, nothing. I, I shouldn't bother you with it. It's no big deal," she said as she started crying hysterically.

"What? Tell me what it is."

She paused and took a deep breath. "Perry, I'm in trouble. I need money."

"What kind of trouble? How much?"

"Fuck Perry! Does it matter what kind? It's the fuckin' kind that's gonna get me fucked if I don't get money, like now!"

"Well what, you want me to lend you some?"

She got pissed. "I knew I shouldn't have asked you, Perry. I knew that if it came down to it you'd be full of shit just like everyone else."

"I'm not full of—"

"Yes you are. Do you think that the other night meant nothing? I made love to you because I like you. But I guess to you it was just sex, huh."

"No…I like you, too."

"So then help me out, Perry." She pulled up close and kissed me on my neck.

"Okay, I guess I can lend you some…"

"Oh Perry, thank you. Thank you so much," she said kissing and hugging me in the street.

"You're welcome," I said as she hung from my neck. "But, how much? How much do you need? And when will I get it back?"

"A thousand dollars and I can give it to you in a couple of days."

My stomach sank. "A thousand? I thought you needed like a hundred bucks. A thousand, that's a lot of money. I mean…"

"Perry. Do you have it or not? Because if you do, I need it. I'm good for it. You believe me, don't you?" She kissed my still-swollen lip.

"Yeah, I guess. You promise you'll have it for me in a few days?"

"Yeah. Or maybe a week."

She smiled the whole elevator ride up to Alex and Andrea's. I knew Alex was home and I didn't feel right bringing her there so late. But since it was so cold and she was freezing and it was going to take me a few minutes to count the money, I told her that as long as she was quiet she could come up. She started kissing me on the neck as we ascended. I contemplated telling her that I couldn't do it or that I didn't have the money. I didn't feel right about loaning her that much…about loaning her anything, for that matter. Shit. I'd known her for three days. I was afraid to say no. I didn't want her not to like me.

Inside, she stumbled and thumped over the end table by the couch.

"Sshh," I said. She started laughing softly. "Be quiet."

The apartment was pitch black except for the green numbers on the microwave that said 2:37.

"C'mon," I said opening my bedroom door and flipping on the lights. "The money's in here."

"Nah. You go count it. I'll make us a couple of drinks."

"Are you kidding me? My brother is going to kill me. Get in here."

She took off her coat and laid on the bed as I took the shoebox out from under my clothes. I'd been spending money like a fuckin' millionaire but I still had about three grand left out of the forty-six hundred I started with. I counted out a thousand dollars in twenty-dollar bills. She was rolling back and forth on my bed like a little kid. She looked very cute. I counted it once and then again and got a different number so I had to count it again. I got the same number as the first time so I counted it once more to make sure. Perfect. I handed it to her. As she reached for it, I noticed scars all up and down her arm. Both arms. Cut marks. She saw me staring and grabbed the money. Before I let go I said, "Okay, so in a couple of days, right?"

She jumped up and kissed me on the mouth. The bed creaked and scraped along the floor.

"Sshh."

"Sshh," she said, imitating me with her finger over her lips.

"Alright, so, do you want to stay here?" I wanted to spend the night with her but was hoping she'd ask me to come back to her place. I didn't feel right having a girl stay at Alex and Andrea's. It was kind of a fake invite.

"No. I've gotta take care of this," she said, holding up the money. *My money.*

"But you can…"

Here's the invite. Beautiful.

"…walk me out."

Motherfucker.

"Oh. Okay." I couldn't believe she was taking the money and splitting without even asking me to come with her.

"Well, let me just piss first," I said without looking at her.

I was questioning the whole fucking thing as the release of the piss made my eyes water. Who did she owe money to? Was it Shadow Man? Did he know who I was? What was I getting involved in?

I was interrupted by a commotion coming from the other room…screaming…doors slamming.

Shit!

"What the fuck is going on?!" It was Alex at the entrance to my room, looking in. All the lights were on and Andrea was yawning and walking out of their room in a robe.

"Oh shit, I'm sorry Alex. She's with me," I said as he spun around towards me.

"Oh she is? Well then I want you out of here, too!"

"What? Alex, I'm, I'm sorry but I don't think…"

"You *don't think*, Perry!" He was screaming.

"Calm down," Andrea said to him. "Let's just relax and talk

about this."

I couldn't see Ginger behind Alex.

"This is what you're spending your time doing?! Who the fuck is this girl? How dare you bring this into my house!"

"Alex, please," Andrea said. She grabbed his arm.

I thought he was going to hit me he was so mad.

"No." Alex jerked his arm from Andrea's grasp. "He's been running around like a fucking rock star since he got here and now this," he said to her. He turned back towards me, "and now you're bringing drugs into my apartment!"

"What? What drugs?" I said, peering past him into the room to Ginger cowering behind my bed. On the nightstand was a small line of coke and a rolled dollar bill.

"What are you doing?" I said to her.

"What are *you* doing, Perry?" Alex was still fired up. "Parading around with some little coke whore?"

"Alex, please," Andrea said.

Ginger pepped up when she saw me. "Perry, are you going to let him talk to me like that? Huh?"

"You know what Perry? Get your shit and go stay with her."

"Alex, c'mon…"

"Now!"

My eyes started watering. I was hoping I wouldn't cry in front of Ginger. In front of any of them. I walked past Alex. I started throwing all of my stuff into my bullshit bag—my clothes, the shoebox with my money in it, and my sketchpad. He stood at the door and watched. Finally, I reached up to grab the two pictures I'd thumbtacked to the wall a few days earlier. And once again something was different, this time with both pictures. The picture on the left, the one I drew of all of us together after Alex's football game, the one where everyone was happy, where we were all smiling and young and it seemed life couldn't get any better, it was changed. We were, instead of people, alive and rejoicing, we were all…skeletons. My entire family had become four dead creatures built of bone, dust, and nothingness. Confused, I folded it and put it in my bag. Then I reached up for the picture of my mom. The colors were still away but other than that it looked the same. But when I grabbed hold of it, it felt wet. I pulled my hand away and there was blood on my fingers. I wiped my hand on my pants and grabbed the picture again and again I pulled it back and my fingers were covered in blood. I could barely hear Alex telling me to hurry up in the background as I reached for it again. This time I pulled the picture from the wall with both hands and started folding it, but as fast as I could fold, blood poured out of the colorless picture. I bent down next to the bed, blocked from their sight, trying to salvage what was left. Blood was all over my hands and the picture was dissolving. I was on my knees struggling with wet paper, trying to hold it together as it became red mush. I felt hands on my shoulders pulling on me as I stared down at my bloody hands and what was left of the picture. It was just my mom's eyes, covered in blood, staring up at me.

I was on my feet and Alex was screaming and pushing me towards the door of my room. I reached down and grabbed my bag off the bed. Andrea yelled at Alex as he pushed me out past her. He kept pushing me until I fell forward onto my hands and knees. Ginger was in front of me, already in the hall. I crawled like an animal, dragging my bag along the floor with my right hand. As I passed the kitchen counter, a few feet from the exit, I hopped up and grabbed a bottle of very expensive, Big Shot vodka off it. I turned to them, placed the bottom of the bottle under my chin and spun the cap off. I held my hands underneath it as the vodka spilled out and all over them. I flipped my hands over and back and over and back as Alex approached.

"What are you doing, you idiot," he said. "You're ruining the floor!"

"I'm washing the blood off my hands!" I yelled, with my head down, trying to hold the bottle as it spat out its contents.

Alex pushed me back towards the door and the bottle fell and smacked off his precious hardwood floors. It didn't break it just rolled, half empty, towards the door.

I reached down for it and turned to Alex and Andrea and started pouring the vodka all over my face and into my mouth, spitting half of it up and choking on but swallowing the other half. Alex pushed close to me and while I had my head back, punched me in my chest, right in my sternum. I spit up and dropped the bottle. This time it shattered and the rest of the vodka spread out onto his bullshit floor. I fell back from the punch and from the burning pain in my chest. Alex was yelling and Andrea was crying. I spun around, grabbed my bag and fell out into the hall. The door slammed behind me and the whole earth shook.

I staggered down the hallway, leaning on the walls, banging on every door I passed as loud as I could. Dazed, I saw Ginger step onto the elevator. People stuck their heads out of their apartments to see me trudging down the corridor. Nobody said anything. I arrived at the elevator just as it was closing.

"Wait."

Ginger looked at me. "I'm sorry," she said as she disappeared behind the closing doors.

I stood there, baffled. Not knowing what just happened.

I'm sorry? Is she leaving me here? It must be a mistake. The doors must've closed too soon. But she could have stopped them. She let them close. She left with my thousand bucks. Oh man, my money.

I ripped open my backpack and rummaged through it. I found the shoebox and flipped the top off. There was only forty dollars left with a note scribbled on the inside of the shoebox cover.

Forgive me Mercury Man.

Frantically I pressed the buttons for the doors to open. I saw that her elevator was almost at the lobby as my elevator opened. I held all my weight in my legs trying to speed the elevator to the ground. My stomach spun. I ran out of the elevator and onto the street. She was gone.

"Hello," Ocean said through a sea of static.

"Hey man, it's me," I replied, freezing on a payphone, trying to hold back my tears.

"Me who?"

"Perry."

"Oh," he said warming up. "P., how the hell are ya?"

"Um, not so great. I kind of, uh, need a place to crash. So…"

"Say no more P. I'm drinking over on the East Side."

"She stole my money, man. She stole it and, and my brother, he threw me out."

"Shit P., what happened?" Ocean said as I stuttered, giving the play-by-play of the last hour of my life. I inhaled deeply. "It was just like you said. You said she didn't give a fuck about me, that she was just using me. You were right. Oh shit man," I said as I kind of buckled at the knees. "She fucked me, I, I, can't believe it. I really thought she liked me."

"Perry?"

I didn't answer.

"Perry?! Listen. That shit I said, it was just to see what *you* were made of. It wasn't about her at all. Fuck, beautiful or not, that bitch is a piece of garbage. I could have told you that from the start. She's fucked up. What she did isn't about you at all. She would have done it to anybody."

That bar looked like every other bar, with countless bottles of poison on display for human vomit to spend their filthy money on. With a bartender who didn't care but pretended he cared more than anyone could ever care. There were sticky spots and uneven wobbling stools and pictures of Marilyn Monroe, Babe Ruth, and Frank Sinatra—people that mattered, people who are all dead just the same—and endless parades of nobodies talking loudly about sports or politics or suicide but really voicing louder-than-death screams how little they matter to anyone. I was letting my cigarette burn away strands of my arm hair as I swam inside a monstrous glass of whiskey. The smell was unlike anything I had ever smelled before. It rose up into my beaten, lifeless face; my mouth gaped open, my eyes red and never blinking, little hairs peaking out from holes in my skin, wanting to fall out and clog something that's hard to get unclogged.

I am a wax statue.

I started letting the cigarette burn closer and closer to my skin. I wanted to burn for my sins. I needed to suffer. *Please let me burn.* The sting from the fire pressing into my forearm was sickly sexual and fantastic. I loved it.

I am an ashtray.

It was after four A.M. when Ocean grabbed my bag and helped me off my stool. I was slurring and stumbling.

"You know, man, you, you are the man, man," I said.

He was laughing.

"I know, I know. It's very fuckin' funny. But you really are the man, man."

Images came at me. Streetlights, taxicabs, a homeless man, scaffolding, windblown garbage.

He thought I was hysterical as he opened the door with me in one arm and my bag in the other.

"Here's your bed." He threw my stuff on the couch and I followed it, crashing face first into crumbs and suede. "Sleep tight man." He took off his shirt and I saw his tattoo through the clouds.

"Whoa, nice place, big shot."

"It's my uncle's. I sublet it, little shot."

Little shot! He called me little shot because I called him big shot. That's hilarious.

"Hey," I whispered as he walked from room to room getting ready for bed.

"What?"

"Do you know who I am? Huh?"

"Yeah, you're a wasted mess."

"I am the Mercury Man. Did you know that? I am the Mercury Man."

"Go to bed drunk-ass."

I laughed. *Drunk-ass is a funny word.*

He walked away.

"Psst. Psst, one more thing," I said, spinning a million miles an hour in my head.

"Perry, what is it? I'm tired."

I caught myself and stopped the spinning for a second and said what I'd wanted to say to him all night: "Thanks."

He turned out the lights. "You're welcome."

JUNIOR

I dreamed I was running through the woods, being chased by someone carrying a flashlight. The beam shot past me and off the trees in front, lighting my way as well as my pursuers. The branches from the trees pulled my skin from my body. I ran faster. Beneath my skin my blood was silver. I ran faster. Silver fell off my organs as the trees pulled more skin. I ran faster. The skin on my face peeled off. The skin on my hands and arms and legs pulled off. I spun around. The flashlight shone on me. My pursuer's face was hidden. My entire body was Mercury…

The phone was ringing and my world was becoming more real than fake as I jumped up. Ocean walked through the room on the portable. He looked blurry. It was gray outside. The answering machine was blinking the number four. My mouth tasted like all of my teeth died during the night. I jumped up and ran towards the bathroom. I barely made it through the door as I began vomiting, first into the sink and then the toilet. I was heaving violently. Every three seconds, my stomach tried to jump out of my body and crawl away. The white, freezing bathroom floor tile was splattered by my yellow insides. I leaned my head back against the wall; it felt cold on my neck and my spine. I flushed the toilet with my toes to wash away the evil.

Ocean knocked on the door and then opened it before I said anything. "Get dressed. We gotta go," he said. He was serious as hell.

"Why? What's up? Who was on the phone?"

"Jimmy. Something's happened."

Down on the street, he walked quickly and ahead of me, as my headache that had settled in right above my left eye, blew my brains out slowly. He was smoking incessantly as people walking towards us jumped out of his way.

"Hey man, tell me what's going on." I had asked him like five times already.

He didn't answer.

We turned right; the block struck me as being quite familiar. I thought it was the block that Jimmy walked me down after I had left Smoke's place that first night I was in town. After she fucked me *and* fucked me over.

Ocean didn't speak as he flew and I trudged up the four flights of stairs in her building. They may as well have been Everest. I followed him through the door. Jimmy was in the kitchen, along with two girls I'd never seen before. Smoke was sitting Indian-style on her bed, against the window. She was smoking and looking down. She noticed Ocean as he walked in. When she looked up, I could see that she had been crying. *Something bad happened.* He acknowledged Jimmy with a nod and walked right over to Smoke. She threw her arms around him and started crying hysterically. She held him around his neck and nearly pulled him down onto the bed. She wailed and screamed, crying like I had never heard anyone cry before in my life. Not in real life or on television.

"Oh God!"

"It's okay, it's okay," Ocean said in a soft, calming voice that sounded more like Jimmy than Ocean.

"What the fuck is he doing here?" She growled, hoarse as hell. She pointed at me as I stood in the doorway shaking. "Get the fuck out of here! Get out!"

"C'mon Perry," Jimmy said softly, escorting me out into the hall. "She's real upset. Don't take it personally."

Don't take it personally. Bullshit.

"Jimmy, what happened? Is she okay?"

He thought for a moment like he didn't know if he should tell me what it was that they all knew.

"Well, last night, she, uh…" His voice was soft. "She was hanging out at a bar downtown, and…" His eyes got red. I had never seen him like that. He coughed and cleared his throat. "Anyway, she was talking to some guy at the bar and, well, she thinks he put something in her drink. All she really remembers is being dragged into a car…"

I felt sick. Nervous sick. Like I knew what he was going to say and wanted more than anything for it not to be true. I wanted him *not* to say it.

"She tried to fight him off, but he had friends with him and she was barely conscious, so…"

"Oh man." I fell back against the wall as I heard her crying inside the room. "They raped her? Oh God, they raped her?"

Jimmy put his left hand on my shoulder, almost massaging me. Calming me down. He saw how upset I was.

"One of the other tenants found her passed out on the street outside when he went to walk his dog this morning."

"Oh, I'm gonna be sick."

"Easy brother," he said, trying to calm me.

I just plain felt for her. I couldn't imagine what she'd been through. I couldn't believe it.

The crying inside had stopped. Jimmy peaked his head in to make sure it was safe for me to enter. Smoke had gone up the fire escape and onto the roof with her girlfriends. Ocean said she needed air.

"I'm gonna kill him," Ocean said to Jimmy.

Jimmy nodded. "I know."

I couldn't believe it when Ocean said we were leaving Smoke's place. "Shouldn't we stay with her?"

"The girls are here, P. You can stay with them if you want," Ocean said as he started on the stairs, taking them two sometimes three at a time.

"Maybe Perry should stay," Jimmy yelled to Ocean.

"No, I'll come," I stuttered.

"So what are you gonna do to him? Huh?" I asked, walking behind the two of them as they raced down street after street on their way to doing something that I was sure would be unlike anything I'd ever seen. I could barely keep up but didn't want them to stop because I knew that they were only going to stop when they got to where they were going, and I needed to see what was going to happen then. I was sober. I'm freaked when I'm sober. They didn't answer me.

I swallowed and pulled hard on my cigarette.

Ocean was slamming his right fist into his left hand. They were still walking in front of me, blowing through crowds of Big Shots on their timed lunch breaks. They stopped at the corner. The light was red so I caught up.

"Are you really gonna kill him?"

"Yes," Ocean said, looking straight ahead. A car horn blew in my ear and I jumped. "They fuckin' drugged her and then raped her," Ocean said out loud, to anybody who would listen. Several people turned their heads. "They ripped her fuckin' asshole apart. They fuckin' pissed on her. They put cigarettes out on her back and on her arms."

I puked in my mouth, swished it around, and spit it on the street.

"She's got to live with it forever. She's up there, hating herself, wanting to rip her skin off like it was her fault. She fuckin' hates herself right now." Ocean turned to me. "Do you know what that's like?"

I thought I did, but not like that.

"This fuck didn't give her a choice. I'm not gonna give him a choice."

Jimmy spoke. "Perry, what he did last night, it's, it's just about the worst thing in the world. And sometimes, really bad things can only be fixed by worse things. You don't *have* to come with us."

The light changed from red to green. We started walking again. I thought about Smoke. I thought about the pain she felt. She'll probably feel it forever. She was in her apartment, probably wishing she had done something differently last night—a different bar, a different street, anything different. I pictured the motherfucker forcing her down as she squirmed. I pictured his friends holding her as she gasped. I pictured them ripping her panties off. I pictured him forcing his filthy penis inside of her. I pictured one of the others switching places with him and doing it again.

I puked again and swallowed it.

I pictured them laughing their asses off about it. They took something that didn't belong to them. I wanted it to be different. Smoke wanted it to be different.

I wanted him killed.

"There it is," Ocean said, pointing to Bar Deep on the opposite side of the street. He walked across blindly as Jimmy and I followed.

All Smoke remembered was that even though his name was Tommy, everyone was calling him something like Baby or Cutie because he looked very young. Like he had a baby face. She didn't remember the other guys.

I bet that babyface looked a lot different when he started hurting her.

We walked in. Ocean fell back and Jimmy took over as leader. It was 1 P.M. and I didn't think I'd ever been in a bar when it was that light out. It was freaky. Part of being in a bar is being able to hide. Even though they had the shades pulled closed, the light still sneaked through the cracks and I could see the hopeless, drinking as the dust danced inside the beams. *What's the point of being in a bar if everyone can see you?*

Jimmy walked up and, in a soft voice, spoke to the bartender.

"Hey guys. What'dya need?"

"One Merlot, a vodka tonic and a whiskey rocks, please."

I don't know what's going on.

He brought the drinks over and placed each one on a coaster as Ocean and I stood very tensely behind our stools. The thought of drinking made me sick. I grabbed my drink. I slammed it. I *felt* sick.

"Hey man," Jimmy said to the bartender who was barely awake as the four or five sixty-somethings drank the day away, trying to forget.

The bartender turned.

"A friend of mine, he hangs out down here, his name is Tommy."

"Yeah?"

"Well, I lost his number and I really need to get in touch with him. Do you know him?"

"There are a lot of Tommys that come down here."

Jimmy shrugged. "Shit, I'm sure. But this guy has a real baby face. He looks real young."

"Oh you mean Junior."

"Yeah, yeah, Junior."

"How do you know him?" He asked skeptically.

"Um, we went to the same school growing up."

"Yeah?" He didn't believe Jimmy.

"Yeah." Jimmy took some money out of his pocket and pushed it towards the guy. "Do you know where I can find him?"

The bartender took the money. He wrote an address on the back of a business card. "It would drive me nuts, everyone calling me *Junior* all day long. It really would. I think I'd develop some serious self-esteem issues," the bartender said.

Ocean flexed his fists.

"Here's the deli he works at."

"Thanks." Jimmy took a sip of his wine.

They walked out. I drank Ocean's drink and walked out after them.

The subway let us off a few blocks from where Junior worked. I asked Ocean if he thought the police should get involved. I brought it up on the subway and he almost threw me through the glass.

As we approached the deli, Jimmy said, "Perry, why don't you hang out. Out here."

"No." I needed to see it.

Then he turned to Ocean. They stomped out their cigarettes.

Ocean threw open the door and walked the length of the counter, staring through the glass display case to find him. Jimmy followed and I hung back.

"Hey boss. What'll it be?" A young guy with a soft, clean, baby face was waiting at the counter to take Ocean's order.

"Junior?" Ocean said loudly opening his arms wide as if he wanted to embrace him.

"Do I know you?"

Ocean hopped onto the counter and over it in a flash as Junior screamed and fell back. Ocean took him by the head and smashed his face into the microwave. Another employee, an older guy, pulled a carving knife and ran at Ocean's back, ready to sink it into his spine. He stopped when Jimmy flew over the counter, reached into his coat, and pulled out a gigantic, gleaming pistol. The guy stopped in his tracks. Jimmy put the silver dick right into the guy's face, up against his lips, pushing them back. He looked like a fuckin' movie star holding that gun. He is King.

"Put it down," he whispered, looking at the knife.

Ocean had the kid down. He was flailing his arms and biting, and kicking and screaming like a maniac.

"Please, take whatever you want," the older guy said, terrified.

Ocean replied, but not to the older guy. "What I want is for you and your friends to suffer," he said to Junior. He looked down at him. He had him by the hair, with his face mashed up against the cabinets. "What I want is for you to suffer for raping my friend last night. That's what I want."

"What? No, no man," he said, dazed. "That's not how it happened at all. She, she was into it."

"Wrong!"

Ocean slammed his head into the cabinets. Then, with one hand, he pulled him up by his hair and with the other, grabbed a bottle of ketchup off the counter. He proceeded to slam the bottom like a hammer, relentlessly against Junior's face, screaming with every hit, smashing his cheekbones, obliterating them, until finally on one hit, the bottle shattered, exploding and projecting ketchup and glass off of everything within twenty feet. There was so much blood and ketchup that the room had become more red than anything else. Jimmy held the clerk back at gunpoint as he cried and constantly looked away to avoid having to see what was happening.

Jimmy yelled at Ocean. "Take this. Hold this fuck back!"

Ocean dropped Junior who collapsed, limp. He took the gun from Jimmy and held it in the face of the older clerk. While the kid was unconscious or dead or something, Jimmy walked towards him, picked up a jagged piece of the shattered ketchup bottle, and began dragging him, with fresh red ketchup and blood-stained hands, into the back of the store. *He's gonna kill him. I know it. If he's not dead already, Jimmy is gonna kill him.*

I leaned back against the cooler, numb. Everything seemed to be happening in slow motion. I grabbed a beer out of it and started drinking. I felt out of my body. I had to remind myself of what Junior had done to avoid feeling bad for him. Two customers, a white-haired couple, walked in and shrieked in horror at the sight of Ocean with the gun.

"Stop it! I'm calling the police," the old man said.

"Hey," I said to Ocean. "Let's go."

"Go get him!" Ocean hollered at me. "Go!"

I dragged my feet towards the entrance to the kitchen. *I am freaked about what I'm going to see behind the door and never, ever being able to forget it.* I peered through the tiny porthole and saw Jimmy facing me, standing over Junior, holding his upper body up by the collar of his shirt. Junior looked lifeless, his arms at his sides, dangling, and his head bent back, worshipping gravity. Jimmy was pulling the bloody piece of glass away from Junior's face when he caught me staring at him. He looked like a wild animal, covered in blood, teeth gnashed, standing over his prey. He let go of Junior and his body slammed. He started walking towards me as I stumbled back and away from the door.

Jimmy emerged covered in red. The couple shrieked again at the sight of him. He *is* King. He threw the bloodied piece of glass down on the ground and it shattered. It was broken already but still it broke more. He pulled his shirtsleeves over his hands to cover them.

Ocean put the gun inside his coat and hopped the counter.

And with that, we were gone.

Paper Airplane

They talked as I walked inside a coma. I felt snot drip out of my nose but when I wiped it on my sleeve, it smeared red. I was bleeding from all the coke.

"We may have to lay low for a while," Jimmy said.

"I know," Ocean replied.

"That bartender, he saw us. He saw me."

"I know."

"And those people and that clerk, in the deli. They saw us all."

"I know," Ocean said more emphatically than before. "I knew everything was gonna change. I just didn't think it was going to be today."

Jimmy spoke. "Don't worry about it, Perry. No one is gonna care about you. You didn't do anything. As for us…"

Ocean snapped. "He was still there. That's all that matters."

"Well, I'm just saying, he shouldn't worry. That's all. I'm looking out for him."

"Right, right," Ocean said sarcastically as we kept walking. "You know…you can't keep pretending that this guy is Paul."

"What'ya talking about?"

"Who's Paul?" I asked.

"*You treat Perry like he's fuckin' Paul,*" Ocean said, emphasizing each word.

"I like Perry. That's why I treat him the way I do. That's it."

"I can't even deal with this anymore. I like Perry, too, but you gotta admit that he's the spitting image of Paul, right."

"Who's Paul?" I asked again.

"You're crazy," Jimmy said.

"*Really, really.* I'm crazy, huh? From the day you met this guy you've been treating him like a little fuckin' kid. Treating him the same way you wish you treated Paul all those years."

"Bullshit."

"Who's Paul, Jimmy?"

"Yeah, Jimmy, who's Paul?" Ocean said, mimicking me like the cocksucker that only he could be.

"Fuck off."

"Hey Jimmy. Tell Perry who Paul is...*was.*"

Jimmy just started walking faster.

Ocean carried on. "Perry, don't you think it's weird how you came here and all of a sudden you're a fuckin' superstar? You got all these new friends and you're hanging out at parties..."

"Jimmy, who's Paul?" I asked again.

"Paul is Jimmy's little brother, Perry. And you look exactly fuckin' like him."

"You got a little brother?" I asked, even though he wasn't looking at me and could probably barely hear me because he had moved so far ahead of us.

Jimmy stopped in the middle of the street.

"Jimmy, you got a little brother named Paul?" I asked again.

Jimmy threw up his covered right arm. A cab swerved across three lanes to pick him up. He opened the door and looked at me.

"I used to," he said and hopped in the cab.

Ocean was cleaning up and showering. He had just put his fist through the wall in two spots. He told me that he better not see me when he got out. He was in a fuckin' crazy rage. I couldn't even talk to him. He left his stained clothes by the door. I was organizing all of my things in slow motion. My hands were shaking so bad. I was trying to pack my shit and disappear before Ocean got out.

I am a witness. I need to be eliminated.

I guzzled half a bottle of the whiskey I'd stolen from the Big Shot the other night. It calmed my nerves. I threw the last of my things into my bag and put my weight on them so I could zip up. I heard the water screaming from the nozzle, pelting Ocean as he washed off his sins. I knew I'd miss him. I also knew it was time to leave. I took one last look around and walked out.

I vomited on the stairwell of his building. Whiskey and blood and dead pieces of my stomach. I needed food. I didn't want to eat, but the black hole in my stomach was expanding and sucking the rest of me into it.

The pizza burned the top of my mouth just like I knew it would. The dick behind the counter with the lame-ass moustache kept it in the oven too long. I held it on my tongue with my mouth wide open, sucking air in and out, trying to cool it down to the point of being able to swallow it and not having to spit it back out onto my grease-stained paper plate. Either way, I knew that when it was all over, I'd have a burnt skin flap hanging from the roof of my mouth. I put the slice down and ran my fingers through my hair, along my scalp, applying pressure to my still-throbbing skull. Again I did it, but this time held my hands on my head and nearly collapsed into them as my elbows held me up on the table.

I finished my slice and washed it down with whiskey from inside my coat. I threw my bag over my shoulder, grabbed my garbage, and with a runny, sometimes bloody nose and wet eyes, began walking out of the pizza place. I knew I'd never see any of them again. Ocean, Smoke, Ginger, or Jimmy.

I wonder if they'll miss me?

I made up my mind. I had barely any money left, no family, no friends, and no hope. This life was filled with pain and hurt and addiction and destruction and death; I couldn't deal anymore. I needed to find a motel room.

I was almost run down in the doorway by two older men dressed in black. I dropped my trash next to the overflowing brown garbage can. They didn't care. They didn't even fuckin' acknowledge me. As I kneeled down to pick up my trash I heard the men talking to Mister Moustache behind the counter.

"…yeah, about six-five or six-six. Brown eyes, brown hair. He's got a tattoo on his neck…"

"Oh yeah, he's in here all the time. I think he lives in one of those buildings across the street."

They were talking about Ocean.

"Hey, what'd he do? Huh?" Mister Moustache asked.

I walked out. I needed to warn him. But *I can't. I can't get involved. It's over. That's it.*

I wheezed as I ran up the stairs inside Ocean's building. My bag had bricks in it. The cops would be checking all the buildings on the whole block after Mister Moustache tipped them off. In fact, they were probably calling for backup right then. I slipped and my shin slammed into the stairs. A Hipster couple with a baby were coming down towards me. I stepped back to let them by. They smiled. Don't even get me started on people and their Hipster babies. I flew off of the top step and around the corner.

I banged on his door.

He didn't answer.

"Yo! Yo!" I screamed as I banged, slamming my right fist into his door until I could barely feel either.

Down the hall, a neighbor with pink curlers in her hair peered out of her apartment.

"Go back inside!" I hollered. She did.

I flew back down the stairs. I was barely touching cement as I glided into the lobby. I blew through the front doors and nearly knocked two cops off their feet; they were checking the names on the directory. One jumped back and out of the way as the other stumbled and spun around like a retarded ballerina and nearly fell into the street.

"Whoa," I screamed and threw my hands up into the air. My heart slammed.

"Hold it! Hold it, buddy!" One cop pointed his hand at me. "What's the rush? What's the rush? Huh?"

"I, I'm late, for a train," I squeaked out. I was wheezing.

The ballerina cop who had regained his balance by now, spoke. "It's not him. Relax."

The other cop settled down. "Let me see some I.D."

"Yeah, sure." I gave it to him. My hands shook.

"Perry Patton, huh. Sounds made up." They both laughed.

"So you're going home?"

"Yeah, I, I was in town visiting my aunt and I'm supposed to be on a train out of town in forty-five minutes." They had to know I was lying. I waited for the cuffs to be slapped on me.

They looked at me suspiciously until the ballerina asked, "You know a guy named Mathew Wallace?"

Mathew Wallace. That's Ocean.

"He's about six-five or six-six. And he's got a tattoo…"

"Yeah, he's got a tattoo on his neck, right?"

I had a plan.

The cops perked up. "You know him?"

"I know who he is. He's a fucking psycho. One time he almost beat the shit out of me for spitting on the sidewalk in front of his building. He's crazy."

"Where? Where's his building?" He said, looking around.

"Oh. Right there." I pointed between them to a tenement three buildings away.

"Thanks, kid. Have a safe trip home."

"Thanks."

I needed to find Jimmy. I needed to warn him. I didn't know where he lived but was hoping, as I flew up Smoke's stairwell, that he'd be there. I didn't care that she screamed at me the last time I saw her. I needed to find those guys.

Her apartment door was open.

"Hello," I said softly as I nudged the door open a bit more. "Hello," I repeated, louder this time.

No one answered.

I walked in and had a brief flashback to the morning that I'd woken up there, the morning I'd first met Jimmy. *Why this girl? Why that night? I cannot believe all that's happened simply because I approached her in a bar a few nights ago. What would my life look like now if I never did?*

I noticed that the window was wide open; the wind whipped through the room. I put my arms through the loops in my backpack and climbed out. I stepped cautiously as I ascended the stairs that led to the roof.

I saw Smoke about twenty feet away, sitting on the ledge, facing out, smoking. She had a bottle of white wine with her. It was almost empty.

"Hi," I said.

She didn't acknowledge me.

"Are you alright?" I walked closer.

Again, nothing.

I walked right up behind her. Her legs were hanging over the edge.

"Look, I'm sorry to bother you. I know you don't like me but I think there may be some trouble, I mean for Jimmy. So I'm looking for him."

She laughed kind of hoarsely. "Perry," she said, looking out on the city. "You ever wonder if you really matter?" She inhaled. She had burn marks on her arms. "Do you ever wonder, with all these people, with all their separate lives, and everything, everyone has going on, if *you* matter? Even a little bit?"

"All the time."

She turned to me and handed me her cigarette. I pulled hard and handed it back.

"I don't think the world will care when I'm gone. It doesn't care that I'm *here* and I don't think it will care when I'm not."

She threw her cigarette off the ledge. It disappeared into nothing.

She was right. The realization had been slowly dominating me. Every day, all of my thoughts were consumed by the pointlessness of trudging through a scared life, filled with humiliation and pain, while time hurtles toward a freezing, silent, black, forever. *Nobody cares. I am so aware, now more than ever, that I am going to be dead and I'll be dead forever and that absolutely, positively, nothing will be named after me.*

Smoke stood up on the ledge and turned to me. She was drunk.

"Perry, I *like* you. You said before that you know I don't, but I do."

"Yeah?"

"Yeah," she said as she started walking precariously along the ledge. I followed a few feet in back of her.

"Hey, maybe you should come down," I said.

"Jimmy's gone," she said, ignoring me.

"What?"

"He's gone, Perry. He came here to say goodbye and pick up a couple of his things."

She started crying.

"Where did he go?"

"I don't know. But he's gone. He's fuckin' gone because he had to be a big man! He let Matt the fuckin' psycho influence him!"

"Yeah, but, he only did it because he loves you. He couldn't accept what those guys did to you."

"I know, Perry! But now," she screamed into the sky, "now he's fuckin' gone and I'm left here alone!"

She was standing in front of the moon, crying her eyes out.

"First Paul, then Jimmy…"

"Who's Paul?" I asked. "Jimmy's brother Paul?"

"Yeah Jimmy's brother Paul," she slurred.

"What happened to him?"

"What happened to him? What happened to him Perry, is he died."

I had a huge lump in my throat.

"That's what happens when you slam into a telephone pole at seventy miles an hour," she said under her breath as her words turned into white birds and flew away. "Jimmy didn't take his keys. He should have looked after him but he didn't. That was his little brother and he should have looked after him but he didn't."

She swayed as a horn blew below. I jumped towards her, but

she caught her balance.

"So you guys were pretty close?" I asked, very distracted by the fact that Smoke was drunk and still walking along the ledge of the building.

"*Close?*" she asked sarcastically. "Close, Perry? I loved him. I absolutely fuckin' loved him." She laughed and lit up another cigarette. "He didn't give a damn about me though. I mean, going off and dying right when we were getting serious. He didn't care."

I wasn't breathing. Not at all.

"You know it's like I said, I don't matter. I never did and I never will." She inhaled hard. "You look like him you know."

"That's what Ocean...I mean Matt, said."

"Yep, you almost had me fooled that night we first met."

"I wasn't trying to fool..."

"I know, Perry. I know. I was kind of fooling myself. Just hoping, you know?"

"Oh."

"It doesn't matter though. You guys are the same. You're leaving me just like him and just like Jimmy."

I didn't say anything.

She was looking over the edge, lifting her legs one by one and dangling them over the side.

"I see your bag. You're leaving town, right?"

"Well..."

"Well," she said, imitating me. "It's alright, Perry. You can leave. You don't care about me. So you can leave."

She took a bag of coke out of her back pocket. She was wasted as hell already.

"No, that's not true. I did care about you. I mean I do care, but you were always so mean to me so, so..."

"Hah!" She did a blast off her pinky nail. She leaned towards me. "Perry, let me tell you a secret: I have a very, very low opinion of myself," she garbled out, using her hands to show me just *how low* low was. "I'm *mean* to people to keep them out. It had nothing to do with you. You should remember that."

"Oh," I said, thinking about how I should have grabbed her off of the ledge when I had the chance.

"Still Perry, you were coming up here looking for Jimmy, not for me. You wouldn't have cared if you never ever saw me again. It's just more irrefutable proof that I don't matter even a little bit."

"That's not true," I said. She was really starting to freak me. "I made sure I'd always have you with me. Look, look," I started, looking through my bag for my sketchpad. I began flipping through the scribbled-on pages. I passed pictures of nearly everyone I had met on this trip: Dirtmouth, Snow, Ginger, Jimmy, Ocean, and Smoke. "Here, look, it's a picture of you. Look," I said ripping it out of the pad and handing it to her. "You see, you do matter, to *me*. I cared enough to draw a picture of you."

She *did* matter.

She breathed deep in a daze and bent down so her butt touched the ledge. She wrapped her arms around her knees and let out a bottomless sigh. "I can't believe they raped me."

"I'm sorry."

She looked at the picture and smiled. "Wow. This is very good. It looks a lot like me. Can I keep it?"

"Yes, I have others. Others of you."

"Perry," she said. "Perry, you just made me very happy."

She took the picture and started folding it.

"Great. Now, maybe you can come down from up there?"

She folded the picture into a paper airplane. She licked her forefinger and thumb and ran them along the bottom crease, tightening the fold. She stood up, lifted it above her head, and launched it. It glided beautifully across the black sky.

"You see that, Perry? Do you see that? I can fly."

"What?"

"I can fly Perry. I just proved it."

"Stop joking and come down."

"Uh uh. I'm gonna fly Perry."

She started leaning out over the ledge.

"Stop it! Right fuckin' now! You can't fly! Now come down here!"

She smiled at me and my nervous rage. She lit up another cigarette and took a long drag. She held it and then blew out two lungs full of smoke. "I know Perry. I'm just joking."

I breathed easier, like a weight had been lifted.

"I know I can't fly. In fact…" She paused and smiled again at me. "…I'm counting on that," she said and jumped off the roof.

Brothers

I spun around silent. My knees slammed into the tarred roof and I tried to catch my breath face-down among the antennae and smoke stacks. I heard a commotion below. Cars honking. A police siren. I pulled my bag and sketchpad to me and crawled to the steps.

I fell inside the window; my things scattered along the floor. I walked along the wall into the bathroom. My legs were made of jelly, but not a delicious kind.

The mirror screamed failure and echoed worthless. The water burned.

I heard someone enter. I stuck my head out of the bathroom. Ocean stood there, looking out the window at the mayhem below. I left the water running.

"What are you doing here?"

"Perry, what the fuck is this?"

"You don't understand, the cops, they're looking for you and…"

"What happened to her?"

"She jumped off the roof. I saw it. She did it right in front of me."

"Oh jeez," he said, sitting back onto the bed.

"You think she's dead? She's dead, right?"

He slumped into his belly and hung his head down between his knees. "Perry, it's fifty feet."

"The cops, they're looking for you. There's no time. They were at your building, I…I sent them down the block though."

"I know," he said with his head in his hands. "I saw you. Thanks."

"You saw? Where were…"

"Perry, we got to get out of here. Someone down there is gonna figure out that they should start checking apartments. If they find me, I'm fucked."

"Me, too. I told those cops you lived in a different building than…"

"So we better put your shit away. Here, I'll do it." He began stuffing my things back into my bag. "Go turn off the water."

Ocean walked over to a picture of him and Smoke that hung on the wall. He kissed his index and middle finger of his right hand at the same time and touched them to the picture. He held them there and sighed.

We flew down the stairs. Every time we'd land on a lower floor, we'd see the mayhem Smoke had caused through the metal fenced-in window on the south side of the building. I think she'd be happy that people *had to* care.

"Hey P.," Ocean said as we got to the lobby. "I think we should split up, you know, for your sake. If they see you with me, you're gonna be fucked. Okay?"

"I guess, but where will *you* go?" "I'm not sure, but I need to leave the city."

I wiped my nose. No blood.

Outside, the police had closed the road. Ocean looked out. His eyes got watery. He was crying, looking out on the crowd surrounding Smoke. I think he was crying as much about her as he was about the fact that his world was crumbling. He had the police after him, he was running away from a pretty pathetic life ruled by ego and intimidation, and his friends were all gone.

Except me.

A cop saw us standing in the doorway. He pointed at us and started walking over. My heart jumped. We both stood still. The cop yelled something.

"Perry, meet over at Starlight Diner, across from Cherry Bar," Ocean said out of the corner of his mouth. "Meet me there in two hours." He darted out the door and past the cop. The cop stumbled and began yelling and pointing and running after Ocean. I sneaked out the door and walked the other way down the street. My legs shook like hell. I thought that at any second I'd feel a hand on my back and it'd be over.

I looked back. I saw a white blanket draped over Smoke's body. Cops and medical workers stood around her. That's all she was, a white blanket in the middle of a gawking audience. I wanted to crawl underneath it and sleep next to her.

The rain pummeled me. I smoked. I drank whiskey. I bought a bottle with twelve of my last twenty-five dollars. I wanted coke. Ocean wanted to meet me. I had two hours to kill. Two hours to kill myself. I took out the bottle of pills. I couldn't afford a room. I'd do it here, on the street. People ran past me. I stepped in puddles. Cars honked. I cried. I opened the bottle of pills. The payphone next to me rang. It rang again. I looked around. It rang again. I put the cap back on and answered it.

"Hello," I said.

"Hello." It was a deep, raspy voice. A woman's voice. It sounded familiar. "Just in time huh?"

"In time for what?"

"Oh c'mon, were not gonna play that game, are we?"

"Who is this?"

"You really don't know who this is?"

"No."

"Perry, didn't you learn anything from what just happened?"

"How do you know my name?"

"You told me your name, a few days ago when we met."

"Met…met where?"

"It was your first night in town and…c'mon, you really don't know who this is yet?"

I kind of did know and it was freakin' the shit out of me. It couldn't be possible.

"Smoke?"

"Well that's not my name, Perry, but I know it's what *you* call me."

I heard a police siren. A cop car stopped in the street right in front of me.

"Hey, c'mere," the cop said.

I put the phone to my ear.

"Smoke, I gotta go."

In a soft, raspy voice she said, "Don't do it Perry."

I hung up and looked at the cop.

"C'mere," he said. "Did you just come from a building over on eleventh?"

I didn't answer.

"C'mere!" He was louder, more emphatic. He was stopping traffic. Cars in the distance honked. "Lemme see some I.D."

"Okay," I said. I walked over and reached into my coat. He watched me attentively. I pulled out the bottle of whiskey and threw it him as hard as I could. It slammed the door right below the window and blew up as he ducked for cover. I jumped onto the hood of the car behind him. I leapt to the other side and onto a parked car, slipped, and tumbled backwards onto the back of another parked car. I rolled off and onto the sidewalk and began running as fast as I could.

The soaked air burned my throat. I looked back constantly. I blew through crowds with umbrellas and raincoats. Every one of them was trying to stop me on my way to gaining freedom. I ran on despite having chest pains. The street in front of me started to slant downwards. I moved faster. It slanted more and I moved faster. More and my feet couldn't keep up with my body. More and I went airborne, left the earth and started falling. I fell, screaming the whole way. I plummeted a few feet from the sidewalk. I tried grabbing onto something, anything, but I was falling too fast. My fingers scraped the cement and started bleeding. The buildings had all flipped on their sides. I flew past them as they pointed out like giant hypodermic needles, ready to inject me and leave me for dead. I fell faster and I felt my face being pulled, distorted. I screamed as I fell past crowds of people that for some reason were able to stay on the sidewalk despite it being flipped completely on its side. I plunged faster and faster until my hands and feet burst into flames.

I am one trillion kilo-tons of dynamite exploding in a newborn baby's crib.

The speed was so great that all sound disappeared and everything turned black and I stopped breathing. It was quiet, like the morning when it's snowed the night before. I was at peace.

Something exploded and I slammed into a thick liquid. Honey. I caused a tidal wave when I hit. The honey wave broke and slammed the sideways buildings, swallowing them whole. I ate the honey. It rotted my teeth. It blinded me. I fell beneath it. I drowned.

I woke up in the street, laying in a puddle. I looked around. The sidewalk was back to normal.

The cop was gone.

I ordered a cup of tea and a doughnut. I was a bit early but needed to get off the street. I was losing it. I needed to settle down.

"Coming or going?"

"What?" I asked the waitress as she put my order down.

"The bag. What's the bag for? You coming or going?"

"Oh, uh, going."

"That's too bad. You're kind of cute." She winked as she walked away.

I looked at myself in the reflection on the back of the napkin dispenser. I had black bags around my eyes. I was as pale as white sand in a place I'd never been and never will, and my bottom lip was fat and scabbed.

Kind of cute? She's crazy.

Ocean came in twenty minutes late. He didn't have a bag or any clothes with him. He sat down and his bloodshot eyes blew a hole in my head.

"What's going on..."

"Can I get some service over here?" he screamed, waving his arms at the waitress.

The other customers looked at us, then continued eating.

"Are you crazy?"

"C'mon! A couple of beers for me and my accomplice!" He screamed and started cracking up. He was drunk.

"Are you fucked man? The cops are looking for us."

"Fuck that, P. The cops can't fuck with me. Nobody can fuck with me. I'm invincible."

"That's bullshit."

"Hey! Can I get a fuckin' beer over here?!"

The waitress came over, slowly. "Honey, two beers."

"I don't want one," I said.

"I'm sorry, sir, but my manager says I can't serve you." She was very nervous and her manager, the coward, was hanging out by the register, pretending not to look at us but watching very closely out of the corner of his scared-shitless eyes.

Ocean laughed. I thought he was gonna blow up, but he didn't. "It's Okay, sweetie. I'll be going soon anyway."

She looked at me before she walked away. She didn't wink this time.

"I'm outta here," I said, and started to gather my things.

"Okay, P., but you got something of mine. Give it here and you can go."

"I don't..."

"Give me your bag."

I didn't move. He reached over the table and grabbed it. As I tried to stop him, he pushed me against the sticky plastic seat back and I sunk into it.

"What are you looking for?" I asked, as he fumbled through my bag, throwing half my stuff onto the table.

He was losing patience, breathing deep and moving quickly, his jaw becoming visible through his skin. "Where the fuck is it?"

"Where's what?"

"Perry," he said a bit louder, causing a few people to look over at us. "Perry. You've got about five seconds to stop playing dumb. After those five seconds, I'm gonna bury you."

"I don't know what you're talking about."

He smiled and slapped me across my face with an enormous open hand. My neck snapped. I knocked my tea all over myself;

the saucer fell off the table and exploded. The waitress gasped and all the customers turned to see me with tears running down my face. The slap stung so hard.

"Sit up straight," he said.

I did.

"Now, are you still unsure about what I'm talking about?"

I took a deep breath. "I really don't know what you are talking about. I...I passed out in the street. Someone could've gone through my stuff. Someone could have taken whatever it is you want."

He started laughing. He looked down, leafing through my sketchpad. The tea had soaked it. "What is this?"

"My drawings..."

"I know they're drawings, Perry. But why the fuck am I one of them?"

"Oh, I, I..."

"What Perry? Oh and look, here's Jimmy and, and, who the fuck is this?"

"Oh that's..."

"Shut up," he said as the entire diner listened in.

"Why are you being like this?"

He chuckled. "Perry, are you a fuckin' homo?" He smiled his ass off, loving the fact that he was crushing me. "Is that it? Are you a little fag, Perry?"

"No."

"Bullshit." He held up the sketchbook and showed the pictures to the customers, all of whom were visibly uncomfortable. "You're a little dick sucker!"

"Shut up," I said, under my breath with my head down.

"I should've known! Perry Patton, the little dick sucker!"

"Fuck you." My head stayed down.

He reached forward, grabbed me by my shirt and pulled me down onto the table as the onlookers gasped. My head shook the silverware. "Be careful how you talk to me, Perry. You don't have the girls here to bail you out. I still owe you one for the shot you gave me in the bathroom."

He let me go. "And what's this, fruity?"

He was looking at a picture I had drawn of him from behind with no shirt on. "What is this, faggot?"

"I'm not a fag…It's a picture of your tattoo…" He stared at me. "The one on your back."

He stood up and over me. He was right on top of me, leaning in. My stomach burned. He opened his jacket and removed it. He took off his shirt, still facing me. I lay hiding in my seat. He took a cigarette out of his pack and lit it. He took a deep drag and turned around slowly. He stopped so his back was facing me. I saw his tattoo under the bright diner light. The man in the tattoo, the one I had drawn and been thinking about since I had first seen it, through drunk rain and exhaustion and a drenched tank top, was me. It was unmistakable. I could see it perfectly. The same chin and nose and eyes and everything. A twin. Identical.

He turned back and spun the top of his lighter. A flame was born. He held it up to my sketchpad.

"Please don't. I, have all my work in there," I said with a completely broken voice. "All my drawings, everything."

"Perry, this tattoo on my back is not for you to draw. You don't know anything about it."

He leaned down into me. The flame still burned. "You thought you could replace Paul, didn't you?"

"No…No…I didn't even know who Paul was."

He held the flame up to my book. "You are not Paul, you little fuckin' bitch."

"I'm not trying to be Paul...I swear I'm not."

He let go of the button. The flame disappeared. He dropped his head and leaned his arms on the end of the table, straight out.

"That's who the tattoo is. It's Paul, isn't it?"

He inhaled very deeply. Not cigarette smoke, oxygen.

"You knew Paul, too?"

"Yep," he said. His head was still down. He sighed. "I got the tattoo after he died."

"How'd you know him?" I asked, soft like cotton.

"He was my brother."

Before I could even register what he'd just told me he looked up and said, "Perry, you want to get your money back? Cuz there it goes." He pointed through the glass at Ginger; she walked into Cherry Bar across the street. He grabbed his shirt and jacket and started for the door.

Cowboy Wrestler and Bat Man

I sat numb and dazed at the table. *They're brothers. All three of them…Jimmy, Ocean, and Paul.*

I knew I could leave. I could disappear. Nobody would ever see me again. I could kill myself in the bathroom or in an alley. I could do it. I had the pills. I had the motivation.

I could walk out the door and be gone from this world forever. I could leave things completely unfinished and never really know what was going on.

That's what I've got to do. Without a doubt.

I stuffed my things back into my bag and threw my last ten dollars onto the table. I stumbled through the diner and out onto the street. It was raining pretty hard and some of the water slid down my back, giving me the chills. I hate that.

Inside was the same as it always is inside, choking and stale and hollow. I mingled through the crowd of Big Shots, Dolls, and Hipsters all drinking and smoking just like their parents asked them not to a very long time ago. I smiled when I thought I saw Smoke pass in front of me. I had to remind myself that she was dead and that she'd be dead forever and that nothing would be named after her. I made my way to the back of the bar. Ocean was walking through a door on the wall of the bar that was the same door I'd walked through the night The Never Enders were born. I followed. He turned around and put his index finger vertically over his mouth, indicating that I should be quiet. We walked down the hall in a dream. I was behind him, blocked by his enormity. The tension was bigger than forever and the silence was crushing me. Ginger peeked her head out from a doorway at the end of the hall. I looked around Ocean to see her better and she looked sick at the sight of me. She ducked her head inside and slammed the door.

"She wasn't counting on ever seeing you again, P," Ocean said.

We arrived at the door and stopped.

"P, on the other side of that door is the broad that stole all your money. She's probably scared to death. What are you gonna do?"

I thought about it. It was my chance to make things right. I put my hand on the doorknob and started to turn it…but I stopped. I didn't want to find out why. I didn't want to hear that she didn't care about me. I'd rather leave than hear that.

I turned to Ocean. "I'm going."

"You're going?"

"Yeah. You said it was about her, not me. She can have it. I don't need it. I'm leaving…I'm leaving."

I walked past him and out through the crowd and onto the street. I started crying a bit. A cop car passed by and I ducked inside myself. I didn't have any money besides some change in my bag, or anywhere to go except to the bottom of the world, or any friends except liars and addicts, or any hope, love, faith, or trust. But I did have one family member who'd always be there for me, no matter what.

I reached into my bag and fished out a few quarters. With shaking, freezing cold fingers I dialed my mom.

I leaned into the booth. I could barely stand from everything I'd been doing and doing to myself. The ringing hypnotized me.

It sounded like a toy machine gun, firing for three seconds and stopping for four. My mouth hung open and some saliva dripped out from the sides. I felt like I could fall asleep forever. The phone rang and rang and rang until finally I heard it pick up.

"Hello."

"Hey Mom."

"Perry…I'm worried sick about you. Are you Okay?"

"I'm not sure."

"What's going on? I know you left Alex's apartment, that you went crazy and smashed bottles…"

"I know…I did. I'm sorry."

"Perry, just come home. You don't have to do this."

"Mom, I just saw someone die…and the cops…they're chasing me."

"Perry, please, you need to leave there."

I breathed deep and didn't say anything.

"Perry, you don't want to end up like Smoke, do you?"

I leaned back and titled my head up and exhaled; my breath, an angel, rising heavenward. And then something hit me.

"Mom, what did you just call her?"

She was silent for a second. "Smoke," she said. "Your friend."

"Mom…how do you know that name?"

"You told me, Perry."

"No I didn't," I said. "I wouldn't."

"What difference does it make, Perry? Your life is too important to throw away. You're so young."

"Mom, how do you know the name Smoke?"

A robot lady's voice came over the line. "Please deposit fifty cents for three more minutes."

I reached into my bag and rummaged through with my right hand while holding the receiver with my left. I couldn't find any quarters. Only nickels, dimes, pennies. I could tell without looking, by the size, the weight in my hand.

"Mom, I never told you that I had a friend named Smoke," I said.

The robot lady came back on. "*Please deposit fifty cents for three more minutes.*"

"Mom, how do you know that name? How do you know that name? How do you know that name?"

The robot lady came back on. "*Please deposit fifty cents for three more minutes.*"

"Mom, how do you know that name?!" I screamed into the phone.

There was silence and then she said, "I think you know, Perry. I think you know."

The phone went dead.

I dropped my bag to the street and nearly pulled it apart looking for quarters. I found a couple caught up in a pair of filthy, stinking socks.

I pushed them through the slot and dialed my mom. The robot lady spoke to me, "The number you have reached is no longer in service. Please check the number and dial again." My quarters popped out of the slot.

I tried again. Same voice, same quarters. Again I tried, and again.

I felt sick at the idea of calling Alex, but I knew I had to.
"Hello…hello."
"Hi…it's me," I said. My hands were shaking.
"What do you want?"
Alex was angry.

"I need to ask you a question," I said, my heart thumping inside my throat.

"What Perry? What is it?"

"Alex, when was the last time you talked to Mom?"

He was silent.

"Alex?"

"Perry, are you serious?"

"Yes," I said. "Why wouldn't I be? Why would you ask if I'm serious about that?"

There was silence, thick, heavy as hell silence on the other line.

"Hello," I said. "Alex, Alex?"

I knew what he was going to say. I hoped he wouldn't, I prayed he wouldn't, I couldn't handle it.

"Perry," he said and then waited a second. "Perry, Mom is dead."

Oh God.

My stomach broke open and the acid began flooding my organs, burning them alive.

"No," I whispered. "No."

I couldn't catch my breath.

"Perry, listen. I think part of your problem right now is that you're not accepting what happened. She died, last month. I was there, we had a funeral."

"No…no…no…"

"Mom has been dead for a month Perry." He spoke louder, angrier. "And she was sick for two years. Two years, Perry. She suffered, she died slowly, while you sat around daydreaming and hiding in your room."

I leaned into the phone, my eyes about to burst from my skull, the receiver pressed against my ear, listening, listening.

"I was up there every damn weekend for the past year and you would stay locked in your damn room."

I knew he was right.

"I wanted to help," I whispered. "…I wanted to…I just couldn't believe she would leave me."

"Stop talking about it like she had a choice, Perry. She didn't have a choice."

"I know…I know…"

"I think you should come here. I think you need to speak with—"

I hung up and hung up again and hung up again and again and again and again, until the phone was smashed, with wires and phone parts exposed and my hand was cut and stinging from the impact.

I grabbed my bag, turned, and walked right into Cherry Bar. A few people got in my way and I pushed them aside. Ocean was drinking at the bar. I pointed to him and then to the back and he put his drink down and followed.

I nearly broke the door to the hallway down as I kicked it open. Ocean was right behind me. I ran my bleeding hand along the wall as we made our way towards the room that Ginger thought she could disappear inside.

We got to the door. I put my left hand on the knob and with my right, smeared some blood on the white wall next to the molding. With my index finger I wrote two words in blood.

NO LOVE

I spun the knob and pushed inside.

Metal slammed across my left ear. I spilled backwards into the hall. My ear was buzzing. Ocean hopped over me and into the room. I rolled over and saw the one thing I never thought I'd see, ever. Ocean *turned his back* to whoever or whatever was in that room and *attempted to run out*, back over me. A lead pipe smashed Ocean in the back of the head. It happened in slow motion. He fell to one knee. Again, the arm brought the pipe down into his head. He fell down onto his hands. The pipe cracked the middle of his back. At that moment, the person wielding the pipe stepped out from behind the door. *Shadow Man has found us.* Four sets of legs flooded the hall and surrounded Ocean as he writhed in pain. They dragged him inside. Then one guy ran back out, grabbed me, and pulled me by my hair and throat. He whooped and hollered like a cowboy. He slammed the door behind me.

The room was dark. There was only a dim swinging overhead lamp in the middle of the room. I sensed silver out of the corner of my eye and was whacked across the left side of my face with the pipe. My head fell down and I watched as a stream of blood fell onto the floor. I collapsed into a pile. I was scooped up off the ground and gripped in a full-nelson by a monster of a man. My body hung limp, being held upright by his wrestling grip. Both ears were buzzing; I fell in and out of consciousness. Shadow Man brought the pipe down against the back of Ocean's neck while he lay on the floor. He barely moved as he tried to reach for the door. I had never seen him like that. Vulnerable. Physically vulnerable. He wasn't invincible at all. He took another pipe blow against his lower back and then a shot across his legs. I was too much dead weight for Wrestler to hold, so he let me go. I fell. Another guy who lurked in the shadows stepped up to me and kicked me in the stomach. Blood sprayed from my sick mouth as I fell over and onto my side.

"Leave him alone," a voice with no body cried. "Leave him

alone." Ginger stepped into the light and pointed at Ocean. "It's just *him*. *He's* the one you wanted. You said if I helped you, you'd leave the other one alone. That's what you said!"

I saw the faces of our attackers. Shadow Man had an enormous bandage around a deformed, swollen skull. The Wrestler was as big as Ocean, easily. Cowboy, who hadn't stopped screaming since the beating started, and another guy with a silver bat and a face that didn't matter nearly as much as his silver bat mattered.

"Oh," Shadow Man said. "Leave *this* one alone," he said, slamming the pipe into my back.

"Stop it!" Ginger screamed.

"Stop it, huh?" He slammed me in the back again. "This is the fuckin' baby you were talking to the night *this asshole…*" he slammed the pipe down on Ocean. "…the night this asshole blindsided me. So, I don't think I'll *stop* beating Baby until I am good and ready to stop."

With that, he kicked me right in the nose. It stung and burned through my brain. I reached up and blood swallowed up my hand.

I looked up at Ginger. She was crying. She mouthed the words, "I'm sorry."

She'd been sorry a lot lately.

At this point, all four of them stepped out and over Ocean. They all had shiny weapons. I felt bad for him. He had to know that this could happen with the life he was leading. Still, as I watched him lying on the ground about to be beaten into oblivion, I couldn't help wondering if he thought it would end like this, being beaten to death on the floor of some bar. I saw the tattoo on his neck that said *love life* in a clean, skinny, black writing.

I'm laying here drowning in my own blood, watching my best friend being pummeled by four guys with bleeding, burning metal pipes, and the only thing I'm thinking is thank God they've stopped hitting me.

My mouth is blood and vomit and saliva. My left eye is nearly swollen shut but still I see Ginger, in all her hideousness, disappearing and reappearing inside of thick shadows and blood splatter.

Six days ago, death was all I wanted. It's why I came here. But lying here, crushed, jellylike, gushing on the floor of some roach-infested bar that doesn't matter to anyone, anywhere, I think about what it was like before all this happened. What it was like six days ago, before my experiments with self-destruction spiraled out of control.

Still, with everything that's happening, I'm smiling. I smiling about the thing that I know that none of them know.

You see, the thing that Ocean slapped me about at the diner, the thing he accused me of playing dumb about when I said I didn't know *what* he was looking for in my bag, you see, the thing about that is that I *did* know. I knew exactly what he was talking about and exactly what he was looking for. I thought it was weird how he packed my bag at Smoke's place after she jumped. *That wasn't his style.* I thought it was weird how he said we should split up so the cops wouldn't think I was with him as we left her apartment. *Since when did he care?* He said he wanted to meet up later. *Why? Why risk it?* So the second I left him, I checked my backpack.

The four of them are cocked and ready to inflict a final misery onto Ocean. They are winded from beating him. Still they begin swinging their instruments and the sound of bones breaking rips me to my feet. With a burning, broken nose and blood drenching my clothes I reach into my jacket and pull out a gigantic, gleaming pistol. *Jimmy's* gigantic, gleaming pistol. Jimmy never took it back after they crushed Junior. Ocean had it. He put it in my backpack so he wouldn't get fucked if the cops saw him leaving Smoke's place.

I can barely hold it up it weighs so much. I walk right up to the back of them.

"Get back! Stop!"

They spin to see me, their weapons wet and warm. Cowboy and Bat Man nearly fall over Ocean's broken, twitching body as I push the gun right into their space.

"Whoa, settle down, Baby," Shadow Man says. "We don't need any nervous little baby shooting someone's balls off. C'mon put the gun down," he says as he steps toward me with his hand out. "Give me the gun, Baby. Your gonna hurt yourself."

I step forward and jam the gun right into his throat. He chokes from the pressure of it. "Get the fuck outta here."

"Okay, okay," Shadow Man says. "Let's go. C'mon guys. Baby's got a new toy. Let's go."

They put their pipes and bats under their coats slowly. "C'mon," he says to Ginger, putting his hand out for her to grab on to. She stands back. "C'mon," he says reaching out and ripping her by her hair as she screams, "Perry, help me!"

I can't help her. I can't let myself care. She chose this life.

"Let go of her! Let go of her or I'll shoot!"

Shadow Man lets go of Ginger and stretches his hand fully, showing me how he *really* let go. He smiles at me. "You're fuckin' dead, Baby. You're fuckin' dead." He is gone.

THE MOMENT

Mom told me a story when I was about fourteen years old. It was about these kids that got drunk one freezing November night and stole a sailboat and went out on the lake. The kids must've started horsing around or maybe the boat was just too old but either way, the boat sunk and the kids were never seen again.

They found the boat nearly broken in half washed up on the shore a few days later. Some people thought it was this big tragedy. They cried and put flowers by the lake, gave interviews to the local papers talking about how great the boys were and how they'd never done anything like that before. And other people thought they got what they deserved. Those people didn't really say that out loud, out of respect for the families I guess. But my mom would tell me all the time how people at her job would say things like, "Freakin' morons. That's what they get."

I didn't really have an opinion either way. Sure, I felt bad that they died and yeah, I thought they were kind of stupid for doing what they did, and I also kind of thought Mom exaggerated the story to scare me away from *ever* doing anything like that. But none of that mattered. For me, the more important thing, the thing I became obsessed with, was *the moment*. *The moment* right after the boat went down. When their heads were just above water, about to go under. When they looked at each other and realized that what had started as something relatively harmless had somehow spiraled and spun out of control to the point of becoming the very last thing they would ever do. I pictured them getting sober as hell in that moment. Their limbs numb from the water. Barely being able to breathe from the cold surrounding their chests. I became obsessed with retracing in my mind the steps they had taken. *Obsessed* with the idea of a number of different people and the random events that led to their meeting at the lake, eventually combining to form their very last act. *Obsessed* with the fact that if they had done something, anything differently, they may not have found themselves gulping mouthfuls of freezing, crashing water and horribly missing their loved ones.

Well, right now I can feel and taste the freezing water. Its weight, pummeling me. Right now I miss everyone I've ever met in my whole life like hell.

Ginger floats in front of me. Swimming and flipping about. Speaking with her hands and huge words but I can't hear her. My eyes roll back. I slam onto splintered wood.

"Perry?! Perry?!" Ginger screams as I look up at her beautiful green eyes. "Perry?! We need to get out of here! Perry?!"

I turn my head to the side and catch a glimpse of Ocean's back. It barely looks like him, wet and broken, shaking on the floor. I don't know him like this. Nobody does. I need to help my friend.

I pop up and crawl over to him. His whole body, swollen, and very hot. His hands, up by his head, surrounded by the blood that had poured out of his nose and mouth as he tried in vain to protect himself. I look around the other side of his head towards his face and eyes and think, just for a brief moment, how horrible it would be if he looks nothing like I remember him and the new image replaces all the old ones I have.

The bones of his nose are coming through the skin on his face like spears thrown through a wild animal. His mouth is open and at quick glance I count five teeth, some broken, some not, on the floor in front of him. His skull over his right eye is collapsed like a partially deflated car tire and dark red blood pools in his ear. Finally, through the black that surrounds his eyes, I see what I swear are tears sitting on his lashes, just about to drop.

"Perry, let's go. We've got to get out of here," Ginger says, pulling on my shirt.

I put my face up to his mouth so that my lips are nearly touching his.

"He's breathing. I need to call an ambulance."

"Perry, there's no time. They're not just gonna let us walk out of here. We've gotta go now and hope to God they're not waiting out back for us."

"Give me your phone."

"Perry, if the cops come, they're gonna ask what we're doing here. They're gonna want to question…"

"Give me your fuckin' phone!"

"Hello, nine-one-one."

"Hi, I need an ambulance…"

"You're crazy," Ginger says as I lay down at Ocean's side, holding him and swimming in his blood. It is sticky and thick, like chocolate syrup.

"Jesus, look at you," she says leaning down to me. She takes out a tissue and licks it and begins wiping my face. It turns red after the first stroke as the blood consumes it.

"That's right, in the back room, all the way at the end of the hallway…"

"Get off the phone Perry. They'll come for him. But we need

to go. No cops."

I look up at her. She has my blood on her hands.

"What?" she says.

"Why'd you steal my money?"

She laughs and looks away embarrassedly.

"That's right, the back room, please hurry." Ocean twitches as I hold him and hang up. "It's gonna be alright man," I say as I stroke his back. I'm running my tongue through the holes in my gums left by the teeth that Shadow Man knocked out.

"Perry, listen to me," Ginger says. "Perry, when the ambulance comes, the cops are gonna come with them. They're gonna want to talk to you. They're gonna want to bring you in for questioning. They're gonna call your brother. And what the fuck are you gonna say? Grow the fuck up, Perry! Jesus! Do you know who you've been hanging out with? You think he'd be waiting here if it was you on the floor?"

She points at Ocean's limp body. I don't answer.

"No, Perry! The answer is no! He has no loyalty. The other one has no loyalty," she says pointing towards the door that Shadow Man had exited through, referring to him. "Jimmy has no loyalty. None of them do."

"What's Jimmy got to do with this? He, he left town."

"Ha! Yeah right. Jimmy's never gonna leave. He'll stay here forever...he matters here. He's important. No way he'd leave."

"Yeah but, the cops...and..."

Ocean twitches. I touch his back. His body is colder.

"Perry let's go! The ambulance is coming. They'll find him back here. You don't need to stay."

She kneels down next to me and holds my hand.

I breathe deep and kiss him on his chilly, violet cheek. "Goodbye, Ocean."

She peeks her head out the door. I half expect a bat or a fist to slam her across her face. It doesn't. She pulls me by my hand and we walk down the long hallway and out into the crowded bar. I have my bag slung over my shoulder. I look around for Shadow Man and his crew.

"Keep your head down, Perry. You're a mess," Ginger says.

I am covered in blood and people are noticing. They stare at me, at us, as we weave our way through and toward the front door. I don't put my head down. I just stare right back at them. Lights are flashing through the glass windows in the front and as we near the doors, they are flung open and men and women in uniforms rush in. They push past us as I drop my head. They are going for Ocean. *I hope he's still alive.* We make our way out the door and sneak past the cop cars and the ambulance. I look to my right and I see Dirtmouth. He is drinking from a silver flask. A silver flask with two silver roses engraved on it. *My* silver flask with two roses engraved on it. He sees me. He looks away, embarrassed. *I knew I didn't like that fuckin' guy.* Ginger pulls my arm and under heavy rain, we disappear down a black alley that cut in between the block.

"We can't go back to my place," she says. "It's not safe."

"What makes you think I'm going anywhere with you?"

She stops. "Well, you need to get cleaned up at least and you'll need to *go somewhere* to do that."

"Well, I think I'll go by myself," I say and start to walk off.

"Perry you don't even know where you are. Don't be stupid."

I keep walking.

"Good! Go you fuckin' idiot! You should've never come here to begin with!"

Something inside me snaps. I turn and begin running at her. She freezes. I grab her by the throat and throw her against the brick wall. Her head slams and she covers her face with her hands. I lean in on her.

"What's the message?"

"What?" she squeaks out with her eyes closed.

"The message. You told me that night that I was the messenger. You told me I was sent here. That I was the Mercury Man. What's the message? What's the fucking message?!"

"Perry," she starts, sobbing, "Perry, I really need you."

"Why'd you steal my money? Huh!"

"Oh, I had to. I needed it. I needed to pay him."

"Who? Pay who?"

"Perry you don't understand. Even though he told me to do it, I really did want to. Not at first but during, I, I, really wanted to."

"Do what? Do what?"

"Oh Perry," she says, running her fingers over my top lip.

"What were you told to do…What were you told to do?"

She looks down.

"Have sex with me?"

She nods.

"Who told you to have sex with me?" I ask, squeezing her thin throat in my hands.

"Perry, I really do like you…"

"Who told you?!"

"Jimmy! Jimmy told me!"

I feel my knees buckle and I let go of her throat. "You fucked me because Jimmy told you to?"

"Don't call it that. Don't call it fucking."

"What are you a whore?! Are you a fucking whore?!"

"Fuck you, Perry! Fuck you! You don't know anything about it! How dare you judge me!"

"You stole all my money! You're a fucking hooker! I trusted you and you're a fucking hooker!"

She cries hysterically. "I knew you'd judge me! I knew you'd never understand! I took the money from you so I could get out of his debt! Perry, you saved me."

"You owed the money to Jimmy?"

"Yes, yes Perry. But thanks to you I'm free now. I don't owe him anything anymore. That's the message. That I deserve better than that life. That's the message. And what you gave me is my freedom."

"I didn't give it. You stole it."

"I'm sorry, Perry. I was desperate. I'll pay you back. I will. Even if it takes me a really long time. I swear I will. I want to get clean. I want to have a life, Perry."

I was silent for a second and asked, "Why, I just don't understand why?"

"*Why what*, Perry? Why I'd steal your money or why I'd fuck you just because Jimmy told me to?"

"Both. You're better than that."

She pauses and speaks softly. "I'm not better than that, Perry. I am that."

"Not to me."

My face is a stinging, burning mask that feels like it has been dragged for miles along cold cement behind a speeding vehicle. My pointer and middle fingers on my right hand are at the very least sprained but more likely broken. *I need to get to a hospital.*

"Hey listen," I say. "I don't feel well. I think I should go to a doctor or a hospital or something."

Ginger doesn't acknowledge my voice. She just veers away from me and into a liquor store.

I light up a cigarette. A couple of raindrops slam down on it trying to put it out to no avail. The inhale crushes my insides and when I cough it feels as if all my muscles are dying in a horrible fire. It takes a moment to recover from the first inhale. Just long enough for me to forget exactly what it felt like. I inhale again. It hurts almost as much. I inhale again and hold it. I feel myself dizzy and probably dying inside scraped skin.

In the midst of the torture I catch a glimpse of my reflection in the window of the liquor store. My face is no longer my face. It is swollen and partially deformed from the blows with the pipe. Dried blood forms a terrible circle from my nostrils around my mouth. I pull up close to the glass and smile. Three of my front teeth are gone, back on the floor of the bar, waiting to be swept away and thrown into the trash; a part of me lost forever. I inhale and blow the smoke against the glass. I am inches from it. The smoke leaves my mouth, spreads out, and races across the window, and eventually leaps off and into the black oil sky to join the clouds as they plan their daytime formations.

I imagine my skin peeling away from my bones with each inhalation, leaving me as it will when I am dead and buried in the freezing cold ground. *I know it. I know that I'll be dead and I'll be dead forever and nothing will be named after me.* It is the same for everyone; the exceptions are the heroes, the visionaries, the saviors. They're here so the scum in the street have something to emulate. So we have hope that it is not as pointless as it is becoming all the more evident to me that it is. *I'll never be a hero, a visionary, or a savior. Still, they are all dead just the same. Nobody wins.*

Ginger taps her fingers against the glass and shocks me out of the haze.

"Here," she says and puts a bottle of wine in front of me.

I make a face.

"It's wine, Perry. Have some."

I take a swig. It comes back up.

"I need to see a doctor."

"Perry if you go to a hospital like this they're going to get the cops involved. Don't be a baby. The bleeding's stopped."

I take another swig and what makes it into my mouth burns the holes left by my broken teeth. Some wine dribbles down my chin and I wipe it with my stiff fingers and lick them clean. I take another swig and another. It hurts as much as inhaling the cigarette. I inhale my cigarette. It hurts as much as it feels good. There is an odd comfort in the pain. At least I know what to expect.

We drink as we walk downtown. The wine tastes like roses blended with vanilla. The rain beats us, washing our dead skin off and into the sewer. The street is empty because of the rain. I pull out my dick and began pissing in the doorway of some building, under an awning.

We aren't speaking, just passing the bottle back and forth. I start hating her again. I want to slam the bottle off of her skull. Payback for what she put me through. She starts walking into the park at 14th Street. I follow. I step in water and sink up to my ankles. My socks are drenched. I take a swig. She spins around in front of me as we get a few feet into the park. I walk up to her. She grabs my shirt and pulls me close, kissing me. I push her away. I haven't kissed her in a few days. It's different this time.

I hate that she's fucked other guys. I hate the idea of her being passed around and not stopping it.

She tries to kiss me again.

"Stop it."

"Perry, please, I want to feel you."

My heart is racing.

"Perry, I told you that you were different. I need you to be with me. To care about me."

"What's wrong with just being some whore? That didn't do it for you?"

"Perry, please, please be with me."

She starts crying.

I fuckin' hate her so much right now. I can feel the rage exploding inside me.

"Okay, okay. That's what you want? You want me to *be with* you?"

I begin tearing at her shirt. I rip it open and the rain covers her chest before my mouth makes its way down to her breasts. She pulls my face up to hers and tries to kiss me but I pull away. I won't kiss a whore. I go back to her chest. I'm biting her with broken teeth and begin clawing at her skirt with broken fingers. My weight is too much for her and she stumbles backward and we both fall onto the grass.

"Perry, please kiss me."

I don't answer. I just pull her skirt up and rip her underwear down. I unzip my jeans. "Perry, stop," she says, struggling.

I don't listen. I just maneuver myself so that I can slide inside of her.

"Perry, stop please." She's still crying.

"What's the matter, you don't like me anymore?" I ask, sarcastic as hell.

"Not like this, Perry."

"What, you're a whore, what's wrong with this? Huh?"

"Perry get off me!" she screams, writhing around, trying to slide out from underneath me as I try to get inside of her.

Oh God, I hate her right now.

"How many guys have you fucked?"

"It doesn't fuckin' matter, Perry! Just get the fuck off of me!"

I put my penis up against her. I can feel her warmth.

"Perry! Get off of me! Stop it!"

She is crying hysterically. I am just about to push inside of her. She sighs and her eyes roll back and away from my face. She looks up into the night.

"Okay, Perry, okay. If this is how you want it, if this is going to prove to you that you are different, than do it."

"Fuck you!! Fuck you!!" I jump up and off of her. I grab the empty wine bottle off of the ground, spin around, and launch it into a giant tree that had been witness to the whole thing. It shatters and glass joins rainwater as they both pour down upon me. I start sobbing uncontrollably. I fall to my knees in a huge puddle and cry with my head down.

Choice

"Are you Okay?" I ask as we walk back out on the street. She's ten feet in front of me. She doesn't answer. She stops under an awning and tries in vain to light her cigarette. I catch up to her as she shakes her lighter violently. The fluid is gone but she still gives a last-ditch effort, trying to hold onto something after its time is up.

I take out my lighter and with one stroke, I have fire. She struggles with hers. She doesn't want a light from me but she wants to smoke, so she leans her head over and lights it without looking at me. She inhales and looks up at the sky.

"You can be a real asshole sometimes."

"I know. I'm sorry," I say.

She takes a deep breath and sighs like she is exhaling everything that had just happened. "It's Okay."

"Thanks."

"Do you really want to know how many?" she asks as we walk, this time next to each other and drinking a second bottle of wine she'd bought.

"How many what?"

She chuckles. "How many guys I've been with."

"No."

"It seemed pretty important fifteen minutes ago."

I take a swig. "It's all about coke, right?"

"What?"

"Everything. All this shit. Everything with Jimmy and you. It's all about coke, right?"

"Yeah, pretty much."

We walk for a few moments in silence before she continues. "It seems kind of fucked up to you, right? Everyone being so caught up in it that it makes them go crazy."

I shrug my shoulders.

"Of course it does. It's because you haven't been partying that long, Perry."

"Whad'ya mean?"

"You're not obsessed with it yet. You're just having fun, right?"

"Kind of. I mean I love the way it feels…"

"But you're not obsessed. You're not obsessed because you're new." She inhales. "You know you can always tell how long someone's been partying by the way they talk about it. You find someone who says they *love* cocaine and they *love* getting high then you know they've only been using a short time. But you find someone that's been using for a while and they'll tell you a different story."

We both pull hard on our cigarettes.

"Yeah, what's the story?"

"It's like, going out every night telling yourself, swearing to yourself, *I'm not gonna get high tonight.* And every night finding yourself in some bathroom of some bar or fuckin' party…"

I love when she curses.

"…and you're handing over money that you can't spare to some lowlife, all the while knowing you're gonna hate yourself tomorrow. Because Perry, your hands are shaking and all you're thinking about is feeling different than you're feeling at that moment. You know that a whole new level lies inside that little cellophane package. You get used to going to that level and it makes feeling the old way, well, just plain painful. So you make the call and you go to the bar and you make the exchange all sneaky like, which everybody with eyes sees anyway, and you make some new coke friends or party with some regulars and before you know it the sun is up and you can't believe it happened again."

She pauses for a moment. "You're not there yet, Perry. Be thankful."

"That's it?"

"That's it. That's what it's about. That's what everyone wants. Coke is such bullshit. Inhaling and gagging and dry heaving and then having to use the bathroom immediately because everyone cuts it with ex-lax, mannitol, or some laxative. It's total bullshit, getting high."

We have been walking for quite a while and my face and head are throbbing.

"Where are we going?"

She shrugs off my question like she is thinking real hard on something.

"Are you gonna answer me?"

"You want to know what it's like?"

"What?"

"Cocaine Perry. I mean really using heavy cocaine. It's like… wishing you had the guts to kill yourself every second of every day. You hate your life and yourself and you do absolutely nothing about changing it. It's the worst thing in the whole world using heavy cocaine. Especially when it's no longer a choice. Can you imagine what that's like, hating your life and yourself and doing nothing about changing it?"

"I can," I say. "I can imagine what that's like."

She gets sad. She starts crying and I put my arm around her. She puts her head into my jacket. Thunder slams off the roof of the sky, trying to break free. "Two guys Perry. That's it."

"Two guys what? Only two guys in your whole life?!"

"Not quite." She smiles a bit. "But only two guys since I've been in his debt. It's only been a week. So only two guys that Jimmy told me, well, you know."

"Including me? Am I number two or number three?"

"Number two, Perry. Two guys, including you. One nice guy and one psychopath," she says touching my forehead softly with her hand, right on a huge welt.

"Who? Who's the psycho? The guy at the bar?"

Shadow Man.

"Yes but..."

"You fucked him? The guy that attacked us?"

"Well, your buddy kind of attacked him first."

I can't figure out how the sky can still have more rain to give after all it has given already.

"Who is he?"

She takes a moment before answering. "I think he's the devil."

It's 1:00 A.M. We're drinking a cheap bottle of white wine that we found in the cooler in an all-night deli that we stopped by to get smokes. There is a dog barking. A woman is born from a dark alley onto the street. She asks us for spare change. I give her three cents that I find in my wallet. Ginger tells her to drop dead.

"Can I tell you something?" I ask.

"Sure." She returns her attention to me.

"There is this stupid thing I do. It's stupid, I know."

"What's stupid? What is it?"

"Well, I kind of make up nicknames, well actually, fake names for people after I meet them."

"Really? That is weird."

"Yeah."

"Why do you…"

"I guess it keeps me from getting too close to anyone."

"Oh."

"After my mom got sick, I kind of couldn't deal with reality… and when she died…well that was the worst. I guess making things up about people keeps me distant… You don't understand, right?"

"It can be scary, getting close. People expect things from you if they know you. They want you to act a certain way. That's why I don't get close to anyone. You know."

"Yeah. I'm scared of getting close but I think I'm more afraid of being alone," I said out loud, not really to her.

"I'm afraid of that, too," she said, nearly cutting me off.

"I'm afraid that I don't matter. That I won't matter," I say to the sky.

"I'm afraid that I'll never have a wedding," she says to a puddle.

"I'm afraid people will forget about me after I'm gone…"

"Forget that. Did I say I'm afraid I'll never have a wedding? I'm more afraid that I will have one and right as I'm saying *I do* I'll get sick to my stomach, realizing that this isn't the guy. The right guy…"

"I'm afraid that I don't have a dream. I'm afraid that if I get a dream I won't know what to do to make it come true, and if I figure out what to do to make it come true, I'll be too afraid to actually do it. Sometimes I'd rather hate the world for my circumstance than actually do something about it…"

"I guess out of everything, I'm most afraid that this is it." She shrugs her shoulders. "You know, that this is as good as it gets."

I take a swig.

"So what's mine?"

"What's your what?"

"My nickname silly. What's *my* nickname?"

"I don't want to say. You'll laugh."

"I'm sure I will. What is it?"

"Ginger."

"Hah! Ginger! Hah, hah. That's fuckin' great!"

"I knew you'd laugh."

"Damn right. I mean, Perry, c'mon. *Ginger?*"

"What? I think it fits you. Ginger sounds like a movie star's name and that's what you kind of looked like the first time I saw you."

"I think you've seen too many episodes *of Gilligan's Island.*"

"Hmm."

"It's okay. I've been calling you Claude since we met."

"No way?"

"No, I'm just kidding," she slurs, sounding pretty drunk.

I laugh.

"So Perry, are you at all interested in getting to know the *real me* or is the fantasy of *Ginger* good enough?"

"It's not like that. It's not weird or—"

"Yes, Claude, it is weird."

"Don't call me Claude."

"Don't call me Ginger," she says back, smiling.

"I've never called you that."

"Okay, so let's pretend were meeting for the first time," she says, taking a drink. "I'll start from over there and walk toward you and you can introduce yourself and I'll introduce myself back."

"What's the point? I know your real name..."

"Don't be a dick, Claude. C'mon." She walks ten feet away and spins towards me. "Okay, you ready?"

"I guess."

We walk towards each other until we are face to face. She clears her throat after a few moments of silence. I don't get the hint, so she kicks me in my shin—not hard.

"Oh hello ma'am," I say in an awesome fake voice, deep and almost Southern sounding. "My name is Perry Patton." She starts laughing and so do I. "What's yours?"

"Well hello, Perry," she says in a retarded British accent, the worst British accent I've ever heard. "My name is Vanessa. It's very, very nice to meet a sweet young lad like yourself."

"What's with the accent? You're not English."

We both start cracking up and I kind of think I am an idiot for always pretending about everything. I am having a good time despite the rain and my injuries, and, well, everything with her and everything else.

"Okay, we're here."

"Where?" We stand outside an Irish pub with a cracked gutter, spilling buckets of rain onto the street.

"This is where you're gonna get cleaned up. My friend owns this place. She'll let you use the bathroom. No questions asked. No problem."

"Oh, Okay. Cool,"

She walks inside but before she's *totally* in, she turns to me in the doorway and kisses me on the lips.

"I'll miss you when you go Mercury Man. I'll miss you."

Pink Pill

The television above the bar is painted by police and ambulance lights. Ginger hugs and kisses all the people she knows. I float over and watch the local newsman standing in front of Cherry Bar mouthing the details of Ocean's condition. I want to smash the jukebox so I can hear what he is saying. I watch intently to see if he mouths the word *dead*. Ginger comes over and looks up at the screen and then at me. She pulls me over to meet the bartender.

"Perry, this is Jessica."

Jessica is a tall, slim, blonde woman.

"Hi," I say, still thinking about Ocean.

Jessica says a few things I don't care to hear as I light up a cigarette and sit down at the bar. I catch my reflection in the mirror in between the lights and the liquor. Most of the blood has washed off of my face and onto my shirt from the rain. My head is blue and swollen above my left eye. My nose is twisted slightly towards the bottom and I can't breathe through it. Not at all.

"Perry, Jessica said you can use the bathroom in the office. Didn't you hear her?"

"Yeah, okay, great," I say, not having heard her at all.

"So, do you want to go now?"

"Yeah, sure." I grab my soaked bag and follow Ginger's finger as she points toward a brown door on the back wall.

My bullshit shirt clings to my broken body and I nearly fall down trying to pull it off. It drops to the floor and smacks the beige ceramic tile like an unlucky skydiver. I cup my hands beneath the faucet and splash water up into my face as fast as I can, trying to keep as much water in my hands as possible. Most of it escapes through the cracks between my fingers before it gets to my face. I run my hands through my already soaked hair, slicking it back. My new face looks just like my old face except it's smashed. It doesn't matter anymore.

I kind of like having some missing teeth. It makes me feel like I've been through something. It's always good to have been through something. It gives you credibility. I'm not too worried about any of this stuff. I'm more worried about Ocean and whether or not he's found out by now what it feels like to be young and dead and unloved.

My eyes catch the reflection of silver coming from my belt. Jimmy's gun has become more a part of me than I want to admit. It makes me feel confident and unafraid. It saved Ginger at Cherry Bar. It makes me feel like I matter.

I wrap the gun in a pair of my underwear and place it in my bag. I throw on a dirty shirt that I had crumpled in my bag and throw my old one in the trash. I try in vain to towel dry the soaked legs of the jeans that cling to my exhausted thighs. I reach for my bag and my bottle of pills falls out. They roll under the toilet and stick to the back wall. I bend down and stretch along the wet floor; with my index finger, I pull them back towards me. I am on my knees, holding the pills. I open the cap. I pour ninety pills into my left hand. Tears run down my face. I breathe deep. I hold out my hand. I drop them in the toilet—and flush.

I am going back home. My home. I'm not going to kill myself or drink myself to death or any shit like that. Yeah, I'm depressed, so fuckin' depressed. When my mom died last month, I felt like I died, too. For a million reasons but mostly because I wasn't there for her. Alex was right. I spent all day every day in my room while other people took care of her because I was too much of a coward to help her face what she was going through. Alex was there every weekend. I just never came out to see him. My mom would cry for me to give her morphine. She'd cry through the door. I'd just turn my stereo up. I hated myself so fuckin' much for all of that…I…I tried to destroy myself. I found the Never Enders and we all kind of destroyed ourselves together.

But thinking about it now, thinking about Smoke and Ocean, I'm in no rush to leave this life behind.

My head is pounding and screaming like it is desperately trying to turn itself inside out. And at first I think the noise I hear is coming from inside of it. After a moment, I realize something is happening in the bar…screaming…glass breaking. I peek my head through the door and see Shadow Man. *Fuck*. And he's flanked by his three friends.

He throws Ginger down over a table. It flips on impact. Ginger lands in a bath of broken glass and alcohol. She looks up towards me. Our eyes meet. I swallow and duck back inside the bathroom.

CINNAMON SKY

I feel sick. I lock the door. My hands shake. I dry heave. I'm quiet. There's an open window. I'm leaving. This is out of control. I need to leave. They'll kill me. I embarrassed them. I pulled a fuckin' gun on them. I need to leave.

There's a ledge in front of the window. I crawl up onto it. The window is tiny, barely big enough for me to fit. I peek my head through. I see a dark courtyard. I hold my bag through and stretch my arm down and drop it softly onto the wet ground. I take one last look around and lift myself up and begin to crawl through the window.

I can't leave her...I need to go back.

"Perry!" Ginger screams from the other room. "Help me!!"

I'm stopped halfway through the window. The door nearly blows off the hinges. Shadow Man stands on the other side. I rise on the ledge and face him. He steps towards me. I am three feet above him. He gets close.

"Hello, Baby," he says.

I kick and land a blow right into his mouth. He spits blood. He attacks me, punching his fist through my stomach, nearly exiting through my spine. I bend at the waist, breathless. He grabs my ankles and yanks me down. My head slams on the ledge. He wails on me as I kick back at him while being dragged along the floor. He pulls me into the bar as I cling desperately and in vain to the cold tile.

The bar is cleared out. It is only me and a bloody Ginger sitting on a couch in a dark corner surrounded by Wrestler, Cowboy, and Bat Man. Jessica the bartender is there also. She looks at me. Then she leans down on the bar and snorts a long line of sugar and coughs her ass off. "Sorry, Perry," she chokes out and tosses the keys to Shadow Man.

"Fuck you, Jessica!" Ginger yells.

She walks out and he locks the door behind her. He pulls all the shades closed. He walks slowly behind the bar as his cronies keep an eye on us.

Ginger jumps up and is immediately pushed back down by Wrestler. She screams at Shadow Man. "What the fuck, you psycho! What the fuck are you doing?"

He pours himself a drink and walks over to us. My hands are shaking. He pours some coke onto his hand and snorts it. He coughs. He takes a sip of his drink. "Are you in love?"

"Fuck you," Ginger says.

I don't say anything.

He steps up to Ginger and smacks her across the face. It's so loud it makes me sick. Her head snaps and her hair falls over her face. He pulls up a chair and sits a few inches from her. As her hair falls away, I see her face. It has a huge red handprint on it and she is, for the first time since I've known her, scared. He pours a huge mound of coke onto a CD case and holds it up to her.

"Here, honey," he says.

She just looks at it.

"Here, c'mon."

She looks at me.

He smiles and leans back, letting the coke rest in his lap.

"Are you two in love?" he asks again, this time looking at me.

"Don't say anything, Perry," Ginger snaps.

"C'mon, Baby," he says, looking right at me. "You in love with this whore?"

"Fuck you! Perry, don't answer him!"

He smashes her across the face again, this time with a closed hand. The cocaine flies up in the air. Half of it paints Shadow Man's face and the rest snows down upon a crushed Ginger's back as she falls off the couch. Bat Man holds his weapon across my chest. Shadow Man falls down to his knees and grabs Ginger around the back of the neck and begins rubbing her face against his. He rubs the coke all over her as she resists with closed eyes and small hands.

"Hey, Baby! Are you in love with this whore?" he asks, stuffing her face into the huge bag of coke he had pulled from his jacket. She blows out, spraying white into the air.

"Don't answer him, Perry!"

"C'mon Baby! C'mon Baby! Are you in love with this whore?" he screams, slamming her face repeatedly into cellophane and snowflakes. The bottom of the bag blows out as she coughs and chokes and spits blood across the floor.

"C'mon Baby! C'mon Baby!" he screams, jumping into my face, forcing Bat Man to trip backwards. His lips touch my face as I cringe back. "Baby, are you in love with this whore?" He asks with hot breath on my cheek.

"Shut up, Perry! Shut the fuck up!" she screams.

I swallow hard. "Yes. I love her."

He pulls back, from out of my space. He looks up and rubs his running nose with his sleeve.

"Oh Perry," Ginger says, "you shouldn't have said that."

Ginger is laying down next to him. She smiles at me as the tears paint beige lines through her white and red mask. She closes her eyes. With that, Shadow Man flies over to her and kicks her in the chest. She's nearly lifted off of the ground. She begins writhing around and gasping for breath. I jump up and am immediately smashed across my mouth by Bat Man. I bite my tongue and feel it swell inside my mouth. The blood falls out of my mouth and splashes like a poisoned waterfall off of the cocaine-covered bar floor. Shadow Man punches Ginger in the face, right on her cheekbone and it sounds like a car crash. He begins pulling at her clothes. He tears off her shirt, exposing a red bra covering vanilla skin. It's the same bra and skin I saw earlier in the park. He rips the bra apart from the middle and her breasts fall out, despite her attempt to cover them with her bloody hands.

"Leave her alone!" I scream. Bat Man slams the bat down against my back.

Ginger tries crawling away from Shadow Man, slithering across broken glass to get away. He lunges for her and slams his weight down on top of her. He punches her repeatedly in the back of the head. I scream for him to stop. He begins ripping her skirt off as she squirms.

"Hold her!" he screams at Wrestler, who proceeds to slam one knee onto her upper back. He holds her arms behind her while pushing her face into the floor with his weight. Shadow Man rips her skirt off. Her bare behind is up in the air. Her underwear are soaked and muddy, lying somewhere in the park. She is screaming and it is horrible. Horrible. As bad as it was when mom would moan that she didn't want to die. That she was too scared.

Shadow Man pulls his zipper down and pulls his penis out. I jump up and, despite being slammed across the face by a metal baseball bat, fly at Shadow Man, knocking him down to the floor. My momentum carries me towards the door. I slam into it, shattering the glass with my head. Shards of it stab my lips and cheeks. I turn the deadbolt and rip the door open.

"Help us! Help us!" I scream out onto the dead river.

Cowboy grabs me from behind and drags me back into the bar. He throws me in front of Shadow Man, who winds up and kicks me in my balls while Wrestler holds Ginger down. I gasp and spin around. I vomit wine and pieces of my stomach onto the floor.

Shadow Man comes down into my space as vomit seeps out from my mouth and nostrils. He whispers, "You think I'd let you pull a gun on me and not kill you for it?"

He kisses me on my cheek and stands up. I'd give anything for that gun now. It's in my bag, outside the bathroom window.

Shadow Man makes his way over to Ginger. With my last bit of energy, I twist my head to see her face, smashed and squished under Wrestler's weight.

"Help me," she whispers. "Help me, Perry. Please."

Shadow Man pulls his dick back out and puts it up to her from behind. I can't watch. I turn my head away.

"Twist his head!" Shadow Man screams at Bat Man. "I want him to see this!"

Bat Man nearly breaks my neck as he twists my head towards them.

Shadow Man tries to put himself inside Ginger as she screams for him to stop. Cowboy guzzles whiskey and hollers through the room.

"Help me! Please help me!" She struggles and writhes as much as she can beneath the weight of Wrestler's knee. I feel myself dying inside. She kicks back at Shadow Man and he falls back onto the floor.

"C'mere. Hold her!" he hollers at Bat Man. "Forget him."

Bat Man lets go of me and my head snaps back to its regular position. I'm facing the door, unable to move. Ginger screams for someone, anyone to help her. I can't move. My tears meet the drool on both sides of my mouth and pool under my face and I think that if Shadow Man really is the devil, like Ginger says, this must be hell and hell is horrible.

The commotion behind me becomes the sound of every suffering person on the planet screaming at God.

"Fuck!" Shadow Man screams. I turn to see him slamming his limp dick up and down in his hand. He can't get hard! I turn back towards the front of the bar and begin to crawl towards it.

The door of the bar opens slightly and I see men's shoes. It then opens fully.

A saint walks into the mouth of hell...the *King*...Jimmy.

He walks in slowly, unnoticed. He looks at me briefly. With his right hand, he drops my bag onto the floor. He puts his left hand into his coat and pulls out his gigantic, gleaming pistol. He holds his arm out and towards the horror. I turn to see Wrestler and Bat Man holding Ginger down while Cowboy pours whiskey all over her face. She screams as it makes contact with her cuts. Shadow Man is still struggling with his flaccid dick. He turns toward Jimmy; the sound of the pistol cocking startles him.

His mouth drops as thunder cracks and his head explodes, sending his brains and blood into the air as they turn the sky, just briefly, the color of cinnamon.

His body is blown away from Ginger by the power of the bullet. Bat Man reaches for his weapon, but before he gets to it, Jimmy fires two shots through his throat. He slams down next to me; we're face to face. He gasps for breath as the blood gushes from beneath the fingers of his right hand as he tries to cover the wound.

"Help me," he chokes out.

He reaches for me with the other hand. His eyes are afraid. He convulses. He dies. He'll be dead forever.

Cowboy runs into the bathroom. He trips over the blown-off door. He jumps onto the ledge and slides through the window.

Wrestler freezes. Jimmy walks up to him, the gun still extended. Wrestler puts his hands up.

"Please, please, don't shoot," he begs of Jimmy in a cracked tone.

Jimmy puts the gun to his face. Wrestler has to look away, like his eyes hurt, like he is looking into the sun. They stand like that forever. Then Jimmy waves the gun towards the door and signals for him to leave. He runs like hell, thanking Jimmy the whole way until his voice dissolves into the night.

End

Ginger is in bad shape. She is beaten and weak. She's been bathed in her own blood and showered in Shadow Man's, so she is slippery and hard to hold on to as I lift her onto the couch. I struggle to put her skirt back on. She turns to me with bloody lips and gums and says, "I love you, too."

Jimmy stands by the window looking out through the blinds while Shadow Man and Bat Man's bodies lay motionless on the floor.

Flashing lights appear outside the window. Jimmy smiles, like he's been waiting for them. I don't know how we'll explain the blood or the bodies, but I'm fuckin' happy as hell that it's all over. The police will be inside in a moment and it'll be over.

With that, Jimmy smashes the barrel of the gun through the glass. He begins firing shots—at the police!

I pull Ginger close and duck down. Bullets fly all over as the police return fire. Jimmy sails over the bar and lands on the floor next to us. Everything is silent except for him laughing his ass off. He lights a cigarette and holds it up to my mouth. I pull hard, breaking whatever isn't already broken. I wince.

"Shush," he whispers, putting his hand over my mouth. "Are you alright?" he asks Ginger. "Alright enough to sneak out the bathroom window?"

"What are you talking about?" I ask.

"Yes," Ginger replies.

"Good. Perry, here." He crawls over to my bag and slides it to me.

"Aren't you coming with us?"

"No," Ginger says. "He's staying."

A voice on a bullhorn fills the room. "*Come out, son. Let's not make this any harder than it has to be.*"

Jimmy replies by shooting his last two bullets through the window. He laughs and puts the gun down. He crawls back over to us. He grabs Ginger by the neck and kisses her on the lips. His lips turn red from her blood. Then he turns to me and says, "I can't pretend anymore, Perry. I just can't."

He kisses me on the mouth.

"What are you doing?" I ask.

"C'mon Perry, we're leaving," Ginger says, pulling on my arm and starting to crawl towards the bathroom. "C'mon, it's Okay." she says, as I look at Jimmy, my eyes watering.

"It's Okay," he says. "This is what I want. I can't pretend that I'm happy, that…"

"You don't have to be happy. I'm not happy."

"Perry, everyone I love is gone and it's because of me. Nobody will care. It won't matter."

"No Jimmy, that's what I thought. It's what I wanted, too. But now I know that there is hope. People matter. I miss them. You miss them. They matter." I look at Ginger. "People care."

"I'm sorry, brother."

"C'mon, Perry," Ginger says.

I start to walk backwards, toward the bathroom. Jimmy's eyes are tired and cold, and he has a blood moustache from kissing us. She pulls me by my shirt sleeve as we climb over the broken bathroom door. Jimmy bends down, picks up the empty gun and begins walking around the bar, picking up empty shot glasses. He holds about five in his hand. He smiles at me as Ginger steps up and onto the ledge. She hobbles to the window and slides through. She makes it out.

"C'mon," she hollers.

Jimmy looks at me. I look back. *Goodbye.* I hop up and put my legs through the window. Jimmy turns and begins throwing the shot glasses against all the windows, the broken and

soon-to-be, at the front of the bar. The cops fire back. Jimmy holds his gun high in his left hand and rips the door to the outside open with his right. He points it out at the flashing lights as I fall through the window into Ginger's arms.

I hear shots for a few more endless seconds. Then it stops.

The bed is rolling down a slick tile runway. The nurse has dark hair and a mole on her cheek. I have a tube in my right arm. I try to speak but my mouth doesn't open. I can't get any air into my mouth. I start to freak. I've never been inside a hospital, even when Mom was sick.

I reach for the nurse. I grab her arm and pull her down to me. She yanks her arm away and presses a button on the machine that's feeding my right arm. I feel calm and tired.

"How are you?" Alex asks as I open my eyes.

I can't respond, even if I had something to say. My jaw is wired shut. I reach up and realize that I have tubes up my nose to keep my nostrils open even though I am sure my nose is broken as well.

"Sorry man, don't say anything," he says, watching me struggling. "Get some rest, okay?"

The sky is dark and Alex is still sitting here. He's reading. I am getting his attention. I point to a notepad and pen on the windowsill. He hands it to me. My left arm is in a huge cast.

"How did I get here?" *I write.*

"The cops found you unconscious in the middle of the street."
He says it kind of pissed off. Then he calms down. "They found my number in your pocket."
I hold the pen to the notepad. "What happened to the girl?" *I write*
"There was no girl. You were alone."

The sun burns my eyes. I haven't been outside in a week and a half. Alex says he'll pay for the hospital stay. I thank him…for everything. I write it on a small piece of paper. It makes me embarrassed but still I do it. He has a car service waiting. I see my reflection against the tinted window. I look thin and weak. I duck my head slowly and climb inside the black backseat.

His apartment seems different. He notices me surveying it.
"She left…Andrea…she left."
I grab my pen and jot down, "When?"
"The same night you did. She told me she's been fucking her boss for the last four months and that she wanted to be with him."
Pen goes to paper again. "Are you alright?"
"I'm not sure yet, but I think I will be. It seems like I'm less sad about her leaving than I am about having to be alone…"
I hate being alone.
He got upset.
I write, "I'm sorry Alex."
"It's okay, Perry…You know, you can stay here, until you get better."
I shrug my shoulders and look to see if he really wants me to.

"Yeah, really."

I manage to crack a faint smile. Even with my jaw wired shut, it feels pretty good. He opens a beer and hands me the milkshake he'd bought for me downstairs. We walk out onto the balcony. The sky is clear. People are scurrying about down on the street. He puts his arm around my shoulder.

"Hey, Perry, you should come to visit more often," he says and starts laughing and crying at the same time. I start crying as well. I take a sip of my drink and look up to the sky.

EPILOGUE

I'm sitting on the subway on my way to school and I see someone, a man who looks very familiar. He is sitting directly across from me. He is dressed in old, ripped, filthy clothing. He has a ski cap pulled down over his forehead, almost touching his eyebrows. He has a very young looking face. He is Junior, the guy who raped Smoke almost two years ago. Jesus, I can't believe it's been that long. I can't believe he's alive. I thought Jimmy killed him.

He looks at me. I look away. I look at him. He looks away. He is sitting across from me. We make eye contact. We stare forever. I don't think he remembers me. He stands up.

"Ladies and gentlemen," he says. "I am sorry to bother you on your way to work. I am homeless. I have nothing to eat and nowhere to live. I am not a drug addict or an alcoholic." People ignore him. "I am embarrassed to have to do this but please, if you can spare some change so I can get something to eat I would greatly appreciate it."

He walks to one end of the train car and holds out his hand. No one offers him anything. I reach into my pocket as he makes his way towards me. I fish out about eighty cents. Nobody has given him anything. He steps up to me and we make eye contact again. I hold out my hand to give him the change. He takes off his ski cap and holds it in front of me, upside down. I drop the change in. I look up at his face and my stomach falls out and onto the floor.

He has a word carved into his forehead. The huge scar reads *RAPIST.*

The train doors open. I get up and walk out. He watches me through the glass.

It's been so long since I've thought about any of the Never Enders. It took me a while to get past everything that happened. Smoke and Jimmy are dead. They'll be dead forever and nothing will be named after them. But Ocean, he lived. I saw him on the street one day about five months ago. I was walking home from school and I saw him, right in front of me. I saw him selling hot dogs off a cart on the street. He didn't see me.

He wasn't Ocean like I remember him. His face was droopy and he was at least thirty pounds lighter. He couldn't move his left arm and could barely move his right. He had braces around both of his legs. It took him a few tries to lift either leg when he needed to move. He moved so slowly and stuttered when he spoke. I swear it took him five minutes to give someone a dog and take their money.

I went by his cart every day for the next two weeks. Every time I wanted to say hello, but I never did.

Then one day, he was gone.

Andrea came back to Alex. It turned out her boss left her for someone younger. Alex took her back. I thought he was a sucker at first, but I guess if you really love someone, you can forgive almost anything. I stayed with them for a few months until I healed up and then, with some major help from Alex, started school in the city. I'm studying art and living in the dorms. Alex and I patched everything up and now we get together every Sunday afternoon and hang out.

That leaves Ginger. She moved back home with her folks, about two hours outside the city. We don't talk that much because she says it's too hard. You see, after everything happened, Ginger found out she was pregnant. I didn't even find out until two months after the baby was born. She called me because she thought I should know. I got a paternity test and it proved that the baby's mine. It's a boy. He's fifteen months old. She's been sober since she found out she was pregnant and she seems to be a pretty good mom. I go see him every other weekend, but as far as me and Ginger go, we're just friends. That's as far as it can go. She has trouble being around me because it reminds her of who she was back then and all the fucked-up shit that happened.

It's so amazing when I'm with my son. He is so soft and delicate, and I love him more than I ever thought I could love another human being. He depends on me. I matter so much to him and he matters even more to me. He smiles every time he sees me. And, oh yeah, he looks exactly like me.

As far as I'm concerned, I haven't drank or snorted since the night Jimmy died. I still smoke cigarettes but I am trying to quit. I don't want to get sick or anything and not have all the time I can with my son. It's weird. I spent so much time trying to prove that me being here would never mean anything and that I'd have no legacy and that I wouldn't be remembered, I tried so hard to prove it with my death that I never thought of disproving it with my life. I was so consumed with being forgotten, with being cast aside, with the idea that one day I'd be dead and I'd be dead forever and nothing would be named after me that I all but ensured it by trying to kill myself slowly. I know now that I will be remembered.

Ginger named our son. She named him Perry. He's named after me.

For sales, editorial information, subsidiary rights information or a catalog, please write or phone or e-mail

ibooks
1230 Park Avenue
New York, New York 10128, US
Sales: 1-800-68-BRICK
Tel: 212-427-7139 Fax: 212-860-8852
www.ibooksinc.com
email: bricktower@aol.com.

For sales in the United States, please contact
National Book Network
nbnbooks.com
Orders: 800-462-6420
Fax: 800-338-4550
custserv@nbnbooks.com

For sales in the UK and Europe please contact our
distributor, Gazelle Book Services
Falcon House, Queens Square
Lancaster, LA1 1RN, UK
Tel: (01524) 68765 Fax: (01524) 63232
email: gazelle4go@aol.com.

For Australian and New Zealand sales please contact
Bookwise International
174 Cormack Road, Wingfield, 5013, South Australia
Tel: 61 (0) 419 340056 Fax: 61 (0)8 8268 1010
email: karen.emmerson@bookwise.com.au